OF
DARKNESS

—

Josefine Klougart

TRANSLATED FROM THE DANISH BY
MARTIN AITKEN

DEEP VELLUM PUBLISHING
DALLAS, TEXAS

Deep Vellum Publishing
3000 Commerce St., Dallas, Texas 75226
deepvellum.org · @deepvellum

Deep Vellum Publishing is a 501C3
nonprofit literary arts organization founded in 2013.

The author would like to thank
The Danish Arts Foundation for their support.

ISBN: 978-1-941920-50-3 (paperback) · 978-1-941920-51-0 (ebook)
LIBRARY OF CONGRESS CONTROL NUMBER: 2016959329

—

DANISH ARTS FOUNDATION

This translation has been supported with
a grant from the Danish Arts Foundation.

—

Cover design & typesetting by Anna Zylicz · annazylicz.com

Text set in Bembo, a typeface modeled on typefaces cut by Francesco Griffo
for Aldo Manuzio's printing of *De Aetna* in 1495 in Venice.

Distributed by Consortium Book Sales & Distribution.

Printed in the United States of America on acid-free paper.

"*Assuming that beauty is the distribution of light in the fashion most congenial to one's retina, a tear is an acknowledgment of the retina's, as well as the tear's, failure to retain beauty. On the whole, love comes with the speed of light; separation, with that of sound. It is the deterioration of the greater speed to the lesser that moistens one's eye. Because one is finite, a departure from this place always feels final; leaving it behind is leaving it forever. For leaving is a banishment of the eye to the provinces of the other senses; at best to the crevices and crevasses of the brain. For the eye identifies itself not with the body it belongs to but with the object of its attention. And to the eye, for purely optical reasons, departure is not the body leaving the city but the city abandoning the pupil. Likewise, disappearance of the beloved, especially a gradual one, causes grief no matter who, and for what peripatetic reason, is actually in motion. As the world goes, this city is the eye's beloved. After it, everything is a letdown. A tear is the anticipation of the eye's future.*"

Joseph Brodsky, *Watermark: An Essay on Venice*

All that the eyes see, upon which a gaze falls.

A bag someone places on the floor is: a bag someone places on the floor. All things remain as things, and in that way they are *here*. The room is not disrupted, the chronology is not disrupted—none of its constituent parts have ever been together in that way. The way *I* have always been *she*, and *you* have always been *he*. There isn't necessarily any problem in that. A movement in and out of our bodies, a recollection returned, wandering back and forth between us. Or an anger no one understands. A common reservoir, the increasingly threadlike capillaries of the veins; something proceeding through time, then turning back.

All sounds are quite as distinct. All voices can be heard, and as such none enjoys priority.

A whisper is as clear as a shout. Something serves to amplify the weaker sounds and lengthen the louder ones so that we may hear them. The eyes decide for themselves what they want to observe.

That may be a comfort.

The ceiling, like the spine of a crouching animal. The duality of movement: inwards and outwards; down to the floor, then up. A whisper, and the space expands. Or: a whisper, and the space is compressed.

Not focusing on anything allows *things* to emerge more clearly. The ways in which they connect—with the eyes that see, and the bodies that listen. The fact of the eye requiring distance in order for an image to come together again in a new way.

Plains and skin. Coasts, cuticles.

Such leaps, on all imaginable scales.

Sound and image work on their own, independently. A thing such as *distance*. What can distances be measured against. A sky. A sail we have stretched out between walls. The arching vaults of cathedrals.

And the same goes for time, the past mingling with what is; the salient past that is here, and all that is yet to come: *here*.

The will of the image, and the will of sound. A liberation of the different planes.

For instance:

The image of a beach, a broad belt of sand in panorama. There are no people in sight, we see only beach, sea, sky. Presently we hear two voices, a man and a woman talking. We hear them clearly, their voices rise with ease above the clamour of the waves.

Next, they enter the frame, and the image splits into two images superimposed: the beach before and the beach now; before him and after him, before her and after her; everything that happened *here* will happen *here*—happens *here*. Death is perhaps merely a displacement, the same as silence. A moment's imprudence and then again: *here*.

She opens her eyes and sees the sky through the crown of the tree.
He is standing in the boat, watching the ash settle like a film upon
the sea.
The sea, calmed; the sea, placid now the wind has died.
The ash upon the surface, a rise and fall with the shifting swell,
a soothing hand, a membrane containing all that is fluid.
Like skin covered in burns.
One can no longer see the sky reflected in the sea;
the sky, mirrored no more; the sea, no longer returned by his eyes,
ash, descended upon orbs, lids above the oceans;
and she, as she lies here beneath the tree,
sees the sky dappled by its branches.

The sky is an eye.
Later, she must have been crying—her eyes are bloodshot.

The dying of the wind makes her open her eyes; the sky and the
tree reflected there.
The ash remains; the family must come ashore again,
a tight huddle in the boat,
joined together by the missing of another,

fingers knotted; coming apart and coming together,
filling out a shell.
All to no avail.
Grief, condensing, a pearl in the hand;
music in the next room.

Blue-black canvas. Nothing in the frame but that.
Threadbare canvas, greyed and lame beneath the sun.
The long fingers of the sun counting out different objects
or dabbing at them,
picking out buildings, areas,
illuminating one thing from outside, something else from within.
A few objects can be sufficient.
Illuminating from within.
A movement we understand with our eyes; things reaching out
to you with light.
Or else: our eyes understand differently than the mind; the blun-
dering mind. If one can distinguish and choose, then it is the eyes
one must embrace.
Trusting as the sleepwalker, the world throwing itself before the
eyes.
There is but one light in the world, belonging to the universe;
beaming from the galaxy, radiant in objects and things, passing
through the eye, this way or that; give me your hand, like this.

At first we see only the fabric, an expanse of smokish blue.

After a while we see the movement.

A body breathing beneath the cover.

A body is a crack through which to breathe.

After some time: a sudden adjustment of position, a glimpse of bare skin,

not pale, but not the opposite,

neither rough nor smooth.

The eyes, borrowing and returning.

The eyes borrow the woman and the hills, the sea, the trees,

all that can be seen. The skin, according all movements direction; towards or away.

A person is the only thing that can move a person.

An absence of interest in nature as it is found out there,

or perhaps an interest in what is human in nature.

Nature's humanity, if that's something we can talk about.

Where everything is a directed approach.

What do we do with that which is *without* direction?

Emotion undirected, and a feeling of being left out, always.

It's not combat; there isn't that much left to conquer, not in that sense.

White flags.

She remembered they had talked at length and with gravity, that he had looked at her with resignation and asked what there was to be gained.

There is no movement in the frame.

The woman in the picture. She is lying on her side; we see her knees from above, the clarity of tendons.

Still the syntax of nature exists, the sentence spoken: one voice among several.

Or writing emerged from under limewash, now simply *there*, a gaping wound affording sight of a time other than the one in which you want to be.

We see her body in its entirety;

the landscape a blur in the background,

darkness.

The weave of the fabric, ripples of cotton, alternating dark and light,

the shiny, skin-like quality of its surface.

Metallic, like the sea's metal gleam in mid-morning.

Stillness, because what we see has no borders, no horizon, nothing that reaches an end.

Our field of vision draws the only boundaries, and they are all but imperceptible to us.

Within the frame of our vision, the picture, all that we have:

blue fabric.

We come no closer, only the opposite—we are moving away.

Moving backwards,

losing the pores of the woman's skin, we lose the pores, the fair down of her upper lip that you discovered, the lines of her skin reminding you of some other age—youth, funnily enough, that couldn't quite be placed.

One step at a time, backwards across the fields, upwards through the hills, stumbling, higher still.

More and more dry red earth is seen, more and more of the earth's skin, less of the woman's.

If you can tell the difference, then that's the way it is.

The eye weeps because it is always losing something. Cities. Views. All that the eye no longer sees is lost.

Rapid movements; the business of turning round on a step;

of moving to the other end of the country; grasping a bottle of pills before it hits the floor, nodding and retreating a few despairing paces before sleep in the final metres;

leaving furniture under wraps, yet another summer, houses, apartments, gardens, a street light's sad persistence, reading through all your messages before you wake.

And still: the fact that only what we once saw is close enough to us, so close we can reach out and touch it.

We touch it with our wanting or with our joy. A returning wish to retain something or

merely keep it *here* a moment.

Always the same exchange: what you get, and what you deliver.

What the eyes get, and what they lose. A city to leave.

My body as it was, an apartment, a city.

Before you wake.

The hills, or a jam jar with a single pearl inside.

The details of the skin, the birth spots on your neck and the four pale scars on your legs after the thorn,

that's how I think of it.

With distance all the surfaces become more distinct.

We see the skin as a surface, the sweep of a landscape, the fir trees a belt beneath the sky, the ocean a blue band keeping the sky in place, the glassy sky during spring.

The city is a smear of grey on the peninsula. Extolled cities, how could they ever disappoint;

what wanting does to what is wanted.

You feel the relationship between body and land, as if it were sickness,

you feel it,

what it does to the body,

the place from which understanding something begins.

And the way the body is then an area, a surface, the way the fabric is another.

There are no hierarchies,

there are planes latticing like day and night. Plaiting one's hair tight.

Distances alter when the eye finds a place to attach.

What eye can see in such a way.

We see a leg, a bare ankle.

A brown sandal of the kind I had when I was a child.

Flaxen hair like a bunch of flowers dropped in the sand.

She sleeps and shifts in sleep. The trusting movements that occur in sleep.

Even unnatural sleep,

the sleep of alcohol or medicine, has something touching about it.

Through her thin eyelids we see her eyes.

The unsettled birds.

Ice, twisting itself apart in the bay, the rhythm possessed by nature, seen from somewhere else everything occurs in patterns, there is a rhythm underneath all that is small,

all that is horrific, the tiny hairs below the eyebrow, plucked throughout a life,

to the eyes distance is not crucial the way it is to the person disturbed, to me, who is always

disturbed by details and the seasons. The composition and the rhythm of all things is the same in the smallest and the greatest, distance makes the pattern clearer;

my distance from you, today, as I pass through the city in which we met,

visit the same café and generally;

try to get closer to you.

The rhythm of all things, not as a logical structure, but a sonnet or a tree or a symphony;

simply that, something finding its proper place.

A moment only,

of falling into the world, standing on top of Stabelhøj Hill and leaning back against the wind,

finding a point of balance there,

only then to tumble once more.

Standing there three times in the course of a life.

Balance is no stable state,

but disintegrates, the same way that the proper place vanishes,

the light changing, now once more another, once more again.

We have pulled away and see now her body in one image;

perhaps thinking that motion away must halt before her body

disappears, the way a pore of the skin disappears, burns out.
A feeling of standing with your back against a mountainside,
or with your heels on the edge of a gorge.
The distance becomes greater,
we see more and more of the hill.
The hill, sweeping up from the sea, and in a corner of the picture,
vanishing: this blue heap of fabric, the skin as an area of land
within the interior.

An object falling from a flatbed on the square.
Four or five glances picking it up.
A hand that does. A hand closing around it,
the way the dirt is brushed from it with a corner of a blue scarf,
the careful way it's returned to the pile, as if putting a sleeping
child to its bed,
carried in from the pristine car, through pristine snow, to the
pristine bed.
Firetraps.
The blue light that connects all things.
The daylight's warmth enables the eye to tell apart the figures,
the trees.
It's not the light's intensity, but the light's quality, that makes the
difference.
What is possible, and what is not.
The light in the blue hours. A thought, that everything is about
to perish,
the paint flakes from the vitrine like my skin in summer,

the lines around your eyes and mouth, the day disappears.

But here. Seeing it.

The wrecked body, as it might be found on a road.

That sigh as a body hits the ground,

the air expelled from inside.

The blue light is a chute, the day slides towards night.

Differently in the big cities, it's to do with speed, the traffic

dividing up the sounds in another way.

The blue light enticing with the thought that we are connected now.

We are connected.

The blue light is a blanket that covers the day, a sheet drawn over;

an eyelid drawn down by a finger to cover an eye.

To close a room for the night.

Switch off what is on. Then come back to check.

Make sure.

Pearls begin as grains of sand in oyster shells, later they must be

stringed, or mounted on metal, or placed in a small, soft pouch.

Loose pearls look so abandoned.

Nuts released, exposed in a shatter of broken shells.

Eyes without sockets.

A single shoe, there on the sidewalk.

The roundness that exists in the world is an expression of the

simplest laws of motion.

The laws that govern things that float. The spiralling circles at

a drain.

And the two of us.

When the water runs out, whenever a thing goes to the wall,

motion is rotary.

Shape is a way of communicating, connecting, a way of listening. From all sides.

The crystals that cast back the light, a pine cone drawing glances. The sphere or the circle is the strongest form.

A shape that belongs to all things, in that way connected with winding down as well, united with the winding down of all things. When you let the water out of the tub and a body remains stretched out within it.

Do you remember that.

A core, that is more like a shell we fill up in order to see what we remember.

Mostly I talk about something I miss, the days.

Mostly I believe there is a form into which we two may settle.

Or perhaps not settle at all.

We are travelling at the same speed away from each other.

Everything is moving, at the same distance from a middle.

Something that may put us in touch with the world, on an equal footing, as it were.

He says photographs can be viewed as a kind of frozen music.

Mostly it's more him saying it that occupies her.

The spaces bodies create together are also passages of a kind.

The space between his body and hers is also a room, the room possesses shape.

And is at the same time already a region of memory.

Or at least it shares the shape of a region there.

Magnetism draws the now out of things and connects them with a place already waiting in memory.

A problem for the shape our bodies have found.

Light is impossible to describe. Or—

it has yet to be done.

She stands at the lakes of Copenhagen, on a path colonised by swans

Grey, overgrown cygnets.

It's that time of day, a fade into blue,

like certain fungi when the finger indents the flesh, or bruises on a thigh.

One could say the light draws a boundary, outlining one thing, marginalising another.

That on which the light falls, and that on which it falls no longer—that which exists *without*.

Whatever place it then may find.

What language can be summoned, to describe that which exists outside the light.

All that on which the light does not fall.

With what voice

may we speak of darkness.

The facing light that discomforts us, the eye understanding that we are being conversed, or perhaps: not being conversed at all.

You don't think there's anything left to go back to.

One closes one's eyes, the way a child closes its eyes.

The action of lowering someone else's eyelids.

Had he done so.

On its descent the sun falls level with the eye and the window sills.

She has left the city behind.

The evening comes with warmth here. Her hand clutches her pocket, hanging heavily at the side of the chair.

She places both hands on the table in front of her,
between them.
She turns her head, looks out across the sea.
From the table this can be done.
She has come here to walk and to gather up pebbles.
She collects all sorts of things, and pebbles are a fine, fine thing
indeed.
As if noticing the unique character of some particular example,
those aspects of it deemed seldom—
and the very act of bending down over a pile of pebbles and
choosing between them,
the hand that reaches out and casts its shadow upon them—
is reflective of something both smaller and greater at the same time.
The things you started doing as a child, that you carry on doing
after discovering
they can't really be done.
At least not like that.
To keep something.
Something round that lies in the hand.
Gathered up, and solid.
Pebbles change when removed from the beach. The way a person
is exiled to some other place once something has *passed*.
Or simply changed.
What surrounds us vanishes when we no longer can be seen in
its midst
in a picture.
One endeavours all the time, with photography, everything, draw-
ing up lists, walking the same paths through the city, sitting down

at the same cafés.

To love the same things.

To make love regularly.

To keep a space close to the body like a necessary item of clothing.

Her mother thinks her daughter would be happier

if she got a *proper* job.

One that meant she could *see* people, be of use to others, gain some perspective on things.

But she sees people all the time, in fact she does little else, she tells herself.

The spaces in which we are enclosed encroach upon us and ensheathe us like the thinnest membrane.

He thinks there's something touching about her when she sleeps; when you gather pebbles too. *Touching.*

I am exiled here to this place and mostly I miss everything I knew.

Seeing you in that picture, you and me entwined.

You've left the city to walk and gather up pebbles.

There's something touching about you, when you sleep too.

Like a pebble held in the hand.

Your body has changed,

we have both become saggier in the flesh, bigger and older and more pathetic.

All that sticks to us.

Cat silver in the sunlight; and you discover it and fill your carrier bags until they can hardly be carried at all.

Hardly enough.

Can a person find pleasure in anything

existing in the world.

Some place other than this.

Love possibly, or pearls.

We see an image, a beach in autumn.

The light is special, a singular warmth and milky light.

We see only the beach, and hear two voices.

They are talking.

You can't hear exactly *what* they're saying to each other.

We note they speak with caution that perhaps suggests they don't yet know each other that well.

(...) no, not very often (...)

(...) wish it on my worst enemy (...)

(...) dream about (...)

(...) that someone might see, or, you know, sort of (...)

(laughter)

Exactly, I know!

They stare down at the sand, her short-cut jacket stretches like the canvas of a tent when she buries her hands in her pockets.

(...) Sometimes I'm just in doubt as to whether I fit in. If this is me, or if (...)

(...) A bit like embers that are still warm in the morning, the day after. That's right, yeah.

Small beads of perspiration on the chest, in the groin, the small of the back.

The body fighting against.

He pulls the cover up around his throat with bony fingers.

The empty duvet cover is heavy with warmth and the moisture of sickness.

He turns onto his side, and the cover peels away to expose his back, like when you separate sheets of dampened paper.

He disentangles himself and dumps the cover on the floor, turns onto his back again, his chest rising and falling in complicated rhythm.

He sweats.

We see his chest, the hollows of the collarbones, the hollow of the sternum, descending to where the ribs part, the chest as a basket softened in water, willow malleable to a certain point,

a bead of sweat collecting between the collarbones, then running down to the neck like a rope.

He shifts his head on the pillow, another bead, trickling down his upper arm, travelling a path that follows the muscles exactly like a shadow, or like water finding its most natural course down a mountain.

It soaks into the pillow. He's breathing, we see.

The chest as it rises and falls.

Another bead gathers. Suspended, it trembles.

A hair, piercing the bead like a needle.

A section of the hair is magnified by the bead and we study it.

Any line is infinite, it's all a matter of seeing it up close, a stretch of coast,

the contours of a grain of sand, the skin perhaps.

She thinks about what the ring might have looked like.

A man's ring. A man's ring would be simpler.

If it might still be there, among the ashes, or if it vanished into the
sea, a gleaming iris ring,

when the ashes were scattered;

did the sun gleam,

did the ring fall first; under a cloud of ash

the ring falls.

The bead releases and runs down the back of his arm, into the
shadows there, where we cannot see what becomes of it, out of
frame.

A moist trail left behind on his skin, the area of skin we can see.

It's hard to say if the trail is lighter or darker than the rest of the
skin.

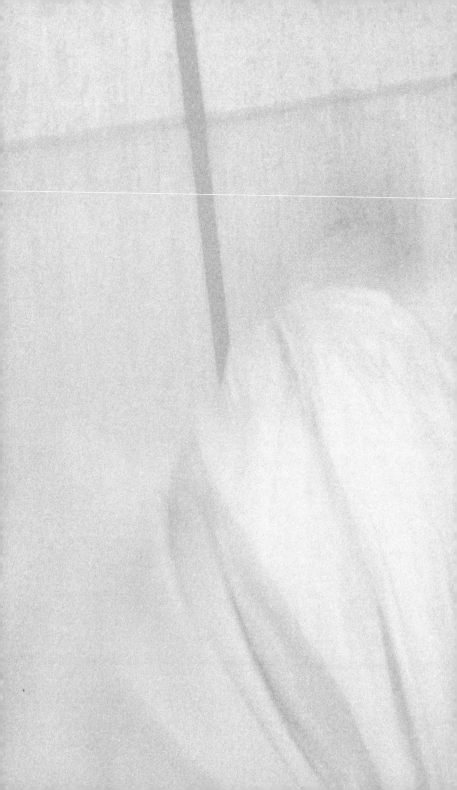

A surfeit of dust, a monument to slowness and cathedrals never completed, built only to stand and witness.

Bulbous yellow of trees.

The tulip trees are blossoming here,

the spring is more advanced,

you say: spring has arrived, you should see the light.

A disorder in the beds.

A soft patch in the lawn where once was a tree, a yielding of the soil.

A chest of drawers, panting green in the room's depths.

What's that you're wearing.

Rooms where the chair has been pulled out in that way, angled into the space.

She pauses in the middle of the floor, in darkness.

His voice, wrenching the skin from my frame in a single move-ment; imperceptibly your breathing has made a fine incision at the nape of my neck, and now you skin me.

What do you want, the man asks her.

The kitchen crackles, and light from the street enfolds the darkness, wrapping it up in its pallid slough.

We view the scene from the doorway, the room is dark, or nearly so.

She has got up to fetch a drink of water or tea, is what we assume.

The question is how much to share,

how much of a *patient* one can be.

How much *human being* one can import into such enterprise.

The sickness had rooted itself within him, his eyes were like that horse's we saw, the black mare down on the farm; if you looked hard enough into its eyes you realised the pupil was quite deformed, spongy in the way of coral, growth upon growth. In the right light you could see it clearly. I held my hand to my mouth, it was a warm day in September when we noticed it first; I rode home gently. It turned out to be nothing. So they said.

It was as if his clothing—his shirt, his jeans—was what kept his body upright, displayed in that way, a thin sheet of skin drawn out over the bones.

Faith is one thing when you're sick, another when you're not.

The flies in the window look more and more like amber in the glow.

"It's touching, what your parents are doing," he says.

"They have to, they love him," she says.

"They love you," he says.

"Same thing," she says.

What price is a person then prepared to pay.

She holds the pearl necklace to her mouth, pressing three pearls inside like a bit.

I don't know what to say to her, but I feel the urge to say something, anything.

The sky is streaked with rain, two different shades of grey, though to you—I imagine—they are alike.

I miss you. Is it okay to say that.

A single water sculpture on the square, water with no outlet, slowly flooding the space. Erosion of the ground on which the city stands.

You drink as if alcohol were the answer to a very important question.

A test that's been given.

The inner lines and the boundaries between the fields.

The transitions from one thing to another.

Help is *near*.

What lies closest to the heart.

Some insane changes in the weather reflect in us, as ways in which we leave the apartment.

When I place my hand on yours, or on your knee, I always get the same feeling, a feeling of not really knowing you. Had we met before, it might have been different. You ask me to do something, get some help, and place a hand on my knee.

There's a common region for caring and prayer and wanting something. Always on the bounds of what is possible.

The things you describe threaten to fall apart.

To break.

Pain can be traumatic because you discover a connection you thought you already knew. The fact of everything being joined and dependent on something else, of our being in danger together, each of us on our own. I kind of knew that, but it's the realisation of it and the fact of believing something only then to be caught out not knowing. Whatever else that might apply to. Brittle glass, small, barely noticeable stone-chips in a window, a small error of calculation, the slightest redistribution of weight, and it surrenders and shatters into pieces.

You have to be as vulnerable as possible.

You have to be as aware as possible. My body and that of the other. You have to look beyond yourself. In such a way you're forever on the brink of dispersing.

Today, while walking in the Botanical Gardens, I didn't tell you, but with each gust of wind I thought I might be blown apart from you and you would have to spend the rest of the afternoon, and the evening too, putting me back together again; I would lie there like a wing spread out in the snow on the slope just here. You could spend days. Feather by feather, a dead bird, wing drawn open against the dark snow, the way snow is dark at the end of winter; the wing extended, the assymetrical form of its stiff quills laid bare, as if pulled out of place. The space between the feathers looks like a negative of the shape, a larger, dark wing that in many ways seems more assembled compared to the wing's lighter spaces. The axes of the body, thought upon thought, what resides outside of thought and language resembles the language in reverse; and quite as diffuse is the darkness. The rhythm of the plumage, eleven sails. We entered the greenhouse and pulled off each other's coats and jumpers and undershirts. I turned, and you unhooked the clasps of my bra, opening it, and there we stood, embracing each other rather awkwardly. Later we would speak of the plant that was blooming there. It flowered for a few days, a week at most, and only once every fifty years, something like that. I could feel your chest very distinctly, rising and falling. I noticed how clear the veins of my body appeared in that light. Or my pale winter skin. I remember wondering if you could sense that I wasn't breathing, and then you said: breathe. It's something you say to make me relax, you claim. Maybe it has to do with your fear of me not really hanging together, that I am already dispersed, spread out behind you. All the living and all the dead. How to make room for oneself in such a world.

Deposition is a term used to describe geological material deposited following *transport*, or as one perhaps should understand it: motion. Three different types of deposit are distinguished: aeolian sediment, consisting of wind deposits; fluvial sediment, deposited by the flow of water; and lacustrine sediment, comprising marine deposits. Glacial sediment, morainic deposits, chemical sediment, salt deposits.

The first image is of the town.

It looks like it once was lashed to the mountainside, and now remains there out of something like—stubbornness or oversight.

The mountains couldn't care less.

The mountains breathe and are blue unreal.

The mountains' hearts possess will in the way of our own.

An interchangeableness, becoming clear as evening arrives, as morning does.

And the ocean:

the way it lies there at the foot of the picture.

Silenced by the morning haze,

which is insistent and—like she—indifferent.

The boats as they lie waiting in the bay.

Their sounds; waves lapping against a hull,

chugging engines, rope that slaps against the masts,

drifting in over the narrow shore, the quay, the main road.

The sounds that cut like blades through the harbour;

the arid earth, blue mountains, an echo lunging up from the sea, into the landscape.

Chopping hoofbeats of the boats—voices of vessels.
The dry moss that yields under her weight,
her feet as they are placed, the roll of heel to forefoot,
sandal straps as they stretch, the foot raised again.
Fig trees, hugging their fruit to their frames.
The sap that leaves the body and the thoughts,
now only these empty pupa remain, to dangle like lanterns—here.
The lips of witnesses have been sewn together.
The violet crowns of the trees;
night's violet teeth.
The distal joints of the fingers becoming loose,
thoughts, becoming loose.

A human being; that one should be lying there.
In the picture, a heap somewhere in the landscape.
Slumped among cypresses, occasional vines, spared or forgotten.

The keeping of something, close to the chest.

He has already felt most of what she says, perhaps even touched
upon it in thought.
An organ, a glossy liver—we breathe on it and wipe it clean.
A connection between the pores of the skin that hoods the nose,
extends across the cheeks,
and the starry firmament here,
these splashes of red on the bench,
a simple lamp switched on,
a mere socket dangling from a cord, a round bulb.

The light inside the room, the only light on the property.
Everything she can see from *here*.

The tree is older than the rest of the world.
A sound reverberating back to us from the time they cultivated the slope.
Speaking from *there*. An olive tree. And beyond the sea's blue tongue as it swallows the strokes of the boat engines,
beneath the surface of the sea—a crackling distortion of sound, and the song of pearls:
a person is lying there, among the shadows of the cypress trees.
It is late, the shadows are longer than the trees that cast them.
Accounts of that kind, a balance sheet.
The slender defence of something perishing and something else remaining.
Small houses, refuge for the yearning.
The blue heap in all that dry red. Between the town and the sea.
A blue patch in a belt of burnt colour. An organ, the liver of the sea. Lying in that way,
motionless. That's how we see it. The sound of the boat engines tears no hole in the haze,
their endless chugging endeavour towards the world.
The haze—a soft, devouring pillow.
We observe its consumption, the passage of prey down through the throat, the thin skin that gives it away.
Nothing exists that can sway such a world,

nothing exists that can sway me anymore, she thinks.

Her hand in the sand, fingers sprouting dead and dry in the sun, tiny twitches,

something dead, pumping life into something alive or—

the fact that all of this exists *at once*.

This is making you ill, he says.

He sits on the bed and gathers her up, the way you pick a pair of sheets up off the floor, and arranges her in his arms.

That's it, that's it, he'll say.

He has a bottle of water; he makes her sit up.

Her eyes are glassy, anaesthetised, their numbed expression, as if the whole eye has only one colour; as if the black, the blue, and the white have been mixed together into something like the colour of dust.

Dust, absorbing all distinctions,

annexing and appropriating all *things*.

You see the water in the bottle, the rings close up, and you see it is a thing of beauty,

all too easily overlooked.

The sea consumes itself again.

Don't be a child now.

You see her dusty eyes, as if they are succumbing and will die.

And she drinks; I acquiesce and drink.

I'm on my way to the beach, I say.

You're on your way to the beach, he repeats.

He sighs, and turns his face to the sky.

I'm on my way to the beach, she says.

Yes, he says, you are, but we need to get you home now.

You're not yourself,

you can't be on your way to the beach, you're not even here.

She is loose-limbed, his cautious rearrangement of her body makes her head loll like a baby's.

Her mouth is open, her upper lip retracted, millimetred back, exposing the white enamel of incisors,

you think to yourself he'll remember this image for a long time;

you think you'll remember it too.

He nods towards the car parked by the side of the road.

It ticks in the heat.

The door on the driver's side is open, a broken wing beckoning.

We need to get you there, first we need to get you there, and you have to help.

Help yourself.

Her eyes keep closing.

You see her lips up close, you see an eye.

An eye, a pair of lips, filling the frame, are all you can see.

Her visible breathing—lungs, and skin.

The breathing of bodies together in sleep.

Birds sail across the sky, dipping and diving, weaving like lengths of cloth being folded, a fan unfurled and opened again, one side then another;

sunlight, bird shadows cast to the ground,

agitated blurs of darkness smudging the land below,

the way the birds themselves shear the light,

the landscape beneath their fragile frames;

the towns.

Our fingers almost touch.

The two people as they sit on the naked plain.

He holds her still. Holds her the way you hold a person you know you soon will miss.

Points of contact are a way of breathing. A finger becomes a mouth as it touches her skin; a mouth that breaks the surface of the sea, to breathe at last—that kind of feeling.

Wide expanses and shining surfaces make us truly fearful.

Being unable to find a place to latch on, find purchase, being unable to make any kind of decision at all.

A point of departure.

It's hard to see how breathing may be shared with a clearing in the forest, or any kind of nature.

At the same time—all surfaces breathe, and one may be encompassed by their respiration.

Basically, there is always some way of *connection*.

Objects in mirror are closer than they appear.

Basically, there is always some way of breathing and surviving, again.

New image.

A shore, the sea behind it. A leaf-green veil of summer shrouds all motion,

muffles all sound. Two people enter the frame, we recognise them, the man and the woman.

They walk along the shore, together, as when we left them, but this is later.

He has drawn her body slightly closer to his.

We observe the motion of their bodies, the way they gradually move closer;

closer still.

We approach at the speed of her body, the speed at which her body moves closer to his.

New image.

Again, the shore, the sea, the sky—this only.

There is a great deal of sky in the frame.

The heat.

The picture shimmers, like when you get out of bed too quickly and the blood drains away.

The shore. Where she was *meant* to be now. If it had only been a matter of—

will.

Like a word running on ahead, the way a blaze takes hold. Trying it out for ourselves.

If it had only been a matter of will she would have been at the sea now, and alone there.

Here, like this.

She sighs.

The waves lap against the sand, a knife scraped across a table,

a lifeless layer of solidified candle wax lifted up, white froth, absorbing into the sand, leaving behind its various remains, soap bubbles or lace,

tiny organisms that vanish down among the grains, a smooth

surface, smoothed like a sheet.

The beach is a new-made bed.

Smoothed sheets, tongues of silky wax, immaculate as a friendship you're not sure if you can introduce to another table or even— another part of the country.

A frailty, reminding us of something we haven't quite the courage to admit is us.

But then once again it's us, thinking like that;

once again our own train of thought bleeding into images, voices.

The fingernails of winter are short.

They have travelled from the winter. The hollow scratching at the doors that is winter, in all its tedium, winter still.

Often the sun is a human voice that addresses you.

A letter that keeps on returning to its sender, who once more turns out to be you.

The will of the skin, the will of the planets.

To have a function or occupy a space that is given.

The night is an unprotected place, like an unexpected clearing in a forest.

When later that afternoon you tell me I'm your best friend, I think of a deer wishing to cross such a bare and treeless place.

You smile and say it's okay.

That kind of unprotected.

If you don't feel the same way, it's okay.

If one were to give the night a voice.

I feel the same about him, but in a way it's worse.

It's still a question of whether it's a kind of crime—reading so much human into nature.

Whether it's our fate to do so.

The seamless movements and transitions, the friction of the bodies' joins.

Everything started with the symbiosis of cells, the way they combined with bacteria that could survive the oxygen,

it's almost the same principle on which poetry works.

And us.

In a way, we're already back at the start, as ever.

The problem of movement always having direction but terminating in itself.

To enter into a symbiosis with the self again, in a new and surprising way.

Eternal rebirth.

He seeps into the ground, his arm dangles from the edge of the bed, legs eaten by light.

A shirt hangs brightly in the wardrobe.

The thought of having a brother you never knew existed.

A wish to be found.

Weighed and measured.

Who do you look like.

Any movement becomes a movement towards her or away.

My paternal grandfather burned his thesis after it was rejected. The only thing I know is that it was about Selma Lagerlöf.

Jerusalem.

One thinks about the fact that some people can gleam the same way as the pupil in a lazy eye

reflects the flash of a camera or some other burst of light.

Just the eye.

A former classmate they'd nearly forgotten.
At first she thinks the darkness belongs to the wall, then realises
it to be human.
All the time, a new past to recall.

We see her face.
A panning shot, a slow, vertical sweep.
Our gaze moving downwards upon her face,
our eyes passing over her, as over a field,
or the way some stories trickle down through a family.
The pores of her skin, tiny dots or shafts leading inside her.
The fairest down.
Too many have died too soon. In my family.
We see her eyes begin to moisten, visible capillaries.
They make a map, rivers entangling in a rhythm we cannot com-
prehend, tide and rain, seasons.
To listen to the slightest shifts.
Snow makes a sound when it falls and settles, as it becomes com-
pressed, as it wanders through the various layers of the world.
Crystals grow. Blood has sound—when the body is punctured,
you can it hear it sing.
Pain is a general term for the feeling that arises when seeing the
person inside you vanish from the body.
Thoughts are a comb you can draw through the body.
Our eyes are fixed upon her, and insistent—they do not rest, but
are constantly busy.
My sister said something one day that made me wonder if she
thought you could get stuck inside a person if you stared at them

for too long.

I thought it naïve, but now I find it more and more likely to be true.

Various fossils.

You tell me you saw an exhibition in Sorø, and that you've seen the oldest *object* in the world.

Older than the universe, you said.

I remember thinking it naïve.

The way your eyes gleamed as you spoke.

Our eyes move slowly down over her face, panning at a speed that seems so very human,

the speed of the body, painstaking and cautious. Eyes are hands. Fingers are the gaze.

We see her eyes, her eyes are in the middle of the picture the whole time.

Eyes are at the centre of what we see all the time, ever a centre of something.

We see only one detail at a time. It's almost impossible to ignore an eye.

The surface becomes taut and shudders; we see reflections of a sky without us.

We are moved.

The sight of the sky in the eye *moves* us.

Like teeth that split in the mouth and double in number, and yet at the same time become: something else.

The mouth becomes another.

Separation does something.

The body is a comb that can be drawn through thoughts.

The body is continually changing into something else. Another body.

The fingernails of night are concealed in the sleeves.

A thread connects the bodies.

We are not here.

Little messages and food between us.

An exchange of something.

The bodies as rooms.

Her mouth is dry. She spreads her legs, he can see right up her skirt.

He lowers his eyes and leaves.

She gathers her legs again.

The night sky may be seen as a weapon,

but everything can.

She drops a tray of plastic beads that spill out in a circle around her.

The glorious child.

Locked rooms next to your own.

What do you want here.

She stands on the balcony, leans out over the railing.

The tall buildings opposite reflect in her eyes.

We stand slightly left of picture, looking in at her from the side.

The canal has been frozen for two weeks. Yesterday the ice broke up, and now the boats are sailing again,

through a carpet of ice, shattered windows or

the ice as verdigrised roofing sheets that burn white and chink like bottles,

yet another street of frost, the canal's long train grating, slipping under and over the cape of ice that casts back the sun in every direction.

She stands on the bridge and stares into the water.

It runs underneath her, and the wind blows.

Sticks and twigs come and disappear.

Garbage passes, an expensive, relentless gloss of plastic,

she holds the railing tight, there is a light and she is standing in the sea in summer.

The water reaches halfway up her thighs.

These threads of light twenty centimetres down, ribbons of tangling gift-wrap, and the sun drilling into the ribbed cheek of the shore.

You wonder how she can stay upright there, how she can avoid being carried away by the river.

The release of a hand, a moment of imprudence and then the

current, gripping her

The movement of her hair.

There is no sound, the image is enough.

To keep something together that can hardly be kept together,

hardly reach.

The sound comes later.

A black screen with sound—her breathing and the murmur of
the channel

is all we get.

Your heart is beating fast, she whispers.

Yes.

She crawls around him, trying to *gain access*.

Like a burglar or someone else, wanting something.

Please stop, he says.

She lies on her back, stiffly, the way you do in the sea when trying to keep afloat.

A thin film of oil on the surface.

The square flooded, and everything enlarges, a biggening of space; the sky is the excavator in a city expanding.

The sound inside an ear. If you ate it, the way a sheet of paper can be crumpled in the hand—whose winter then.

The bush that scrabbles in through the broken pane; the sprouting floor.

That's how they stand.

We hear the waves.

The movement of her hair, like a voice in water.

You look like you're lost in thought. The way you're standing there.
In that way.
Lost in thought.

His eyebrows are bigger and more and more like plants,
her gaze is made of wood.

The tension of the bentwood chairs, the way they curve, like love
that stays the winter.

The idea of surviving oneself.

Two beams of timber thrusting diagonally through the space to
keep him upright.

The piercing gaze in his back that prompts a person onward. Or
a look that binds you to the table, staples your feet to the floor.

She looks up at him. Raises her chin. Slowly.

As if the shadow beneath her jaw is a broad band of dark elastic
that splits and tears when pulled taut, quivering, jawbone sharp
and salient.

You're wasting your time, she says. A voice in the room, saying
just that.

Her voice, and yet from another time.

The ice-breaker lies still in the harbour, or rests in its steel-limbed
cradle in the dock.

She doesn't phone her sisters—it would only ruin things.

The sea, swallowing all.

The sea, making everything its own.

The damming-up of the outermost fields in those years.

The sky, swallowing all.

I can't go on, he sighs.

It's a way of giving her a voice, is what she thinks to herself.

How can you say a thing like that, she asks him in sleep.

She is a body, salvaged from the sea.

She has been without air. This is what we understand.

She splutters.

What were you doing out there.

Or—what were you looking for.

Can a person bring the night up from the bottom of the sea. Can the night be transported into other rooms.

He nods.

He understands, she drinks and brings up a clod of the night.

The night, swallowing all. You'll always have me.

Making everything its own.

The descent of certain sentences into episodes of history.

A pearl inside a clam.

The sea, being the possibility of a hundred thousand pearls.

A bit like the two of us.

And then not.

Have I told you about the hills.

Yes. And I can see them, he says.

He hesitates—

the way you can, he adds after a moment.

She nods—but, she says: have I told you about the hills.

The way they superimpose like faces. Or days.

We see them from above. Skin becomes more skin.

Everything is a question of distance—if you get close enough everything dissolves,

and drawing back again it comes together in new and different ways,

it turns into something one can miss, of which one is *really* fond.

A gradually increasing distance between one thing and another.

An uncertainty as to direction, as to what is moving; who is seeing and what is being seen.

A feeling of being witness to something vanishing.

The eye weeps, its constant loss.

His legs are bent like his thoughts, bent around a very small point or an eye.

The body can be seen as an embracement of air.

Direction in all things.

What will you do about me, he thinks.

His stomach contracts, as if she has gathered together his organs and carries them now across a precious rug.

You see the shadow. The two arms and a bundle being lifted.

The body expiring like light and discolouring all things.

The air can be seen as an embracement of the body.

The moon behind us.

The night, making everything its own, swallowing all.

What can be said of darkness.

The balcony plants have dried out while we've been away.

Dark wood, submerged too long in water.

Birds pecking in the pots.

The green dill, like hands that clutch or else let go. The lavender heads drooping on grey stalks. Something red, glimpsed as you turn, gone when you look back.

Pale furniture, a thistle in the rearmost pot, nature as a kind of darkness inside the city, wrapped around us like a cloak or a shawl.

Nature, making everything its own.

The moon behind us.

Gristle, when cut with scissors,

him shrinking in that way after the transplant.

Face fallen in, as if immersed in a book.

I don't know, she whispered one night, I feel so low.

Not having been there to comfort you.

Sentimental, he said.

All ruins remain intact. If you glance at them quickly, then look away.

You see things the way they were.

At first she thought it was one of the cello's strings that had snapped,

but on closer inspection it was the instrument itself that had split open.

She made a joke about it being his father interfering. But he was actually cut-up about it being broken.

She suddenly remembered once having suggested to him that he made a little box,

in which to collect some of his father's things.

The sister-in-law's brother commits suicide.

It's a month ago now.

She says various things about it when they visit her in their new apartment on the outskirts of the city.

They ask her how things are.

How are you coping.

But she replies without saying anything.

While preparing dinner.

I hear myself saying it probably won't get any *easier*, not even with time.

Some objects might need to be coloured so they can be seen properly when magnified.

An experiment colouring a landscape and moving some of its elements about.

Moving some rocks and scraping some soil aside, for instance.

Making some order visible to the human eye, altering it.

The difference of disturbance.

Some words, entering things and changing them from the inside.

Entering people, changing them from the inside.

Time should be understood like that.

History's medium is the fragment.

The fact of something being moved so we can see.

Alterations of form.

The different speeds of different places, their different movements in time away from a geographical centre.

Beads spilling in a circle around her as she drops the tray.

Form is a way of recognising time.

The organisation of material as a prerequisite of understanding anything at all. I.e. that's where it all starts.

Regardless of his own condition, man is always emerging from a form, and must exist within—a form.

And then another. To mark time.

Alterations of form become crucial.

If undisturbed within the form, one remains young;

she, suddenly, is older, now that he is no longer there.

The eye weeps with the loss of what it is accustomed to seeing.

They huddle around the table like an iris illuminated by a flashlight.

A contraction.

In a way, the only difference is the scale and the sensitivity.

You can only see one thing at a time. Watermarks. The perspective you then select.

The three-dimensional image requires an open viewpoint, one that remains unfocused,

or else one that focuses—on a point beyond the picture, exactly as in literature;

the structures that become apparent appear to us with voice and a form.

The eye's most immediate urge—to see several pictures in one—has to be short-circuited.

Slabs of time, settling as field upon field, or as clouds.

The man and the woman huddled at the table, the iris contracting in the flashlight beam, as if the boundary of light and dark were the boundary of everything.

Simple, self-dependent images and double exposures. Nobody then forgotten.

A white-hot coal.

She puts her fingers in her mouth and goes about like that for days.

We see her as a blur, a figure at his rear.

Mostly she is a body, we see her like that.

The wall is latticed with shadows cast by the timber of windows.

It's hard to tell whether light or darkness is falling into the room.

A voice.

The ocean, brought inside.

Carried from the bay, into the town, across the parched lawn, passing through the branches of the fig tree.

Passing through the branches of the olive tree, the lemon grove.

The birch.

Transported through snow and summer, to slip between the slats of shutters.

I miss her, she says.

Men, taking on the burden, bearing her on; his eyes, bearing her on across the narrow streams,

over the plain beneath the sky's heavy skin.

Her eyes—

skin contracting upon her body like boiled wool.

She is cold, and yet she sweats, perspiration seeps from her pores, a crystal rain of coldness, beading and trickling.

Both of them tremble with rage, shaking—why are we doing this, what are we doing here;

it was your idea, they say in turn, in different ways and with their healthy bodies.

Yes, he says, and sleep descends upon him like a guilty conscience, that's been hidden away.

She toys with ideas about being gone by the time he wakes.

Only then she falls asleep, and will not wake before him.

She dreams.

If only the narrative of dreams could be suffered by others besides the dreamer.

You would see then.

If that were the case, you would see.

The hills bunching up the landscape, the earth here, the grass.

Perhaps nature can be viewed as a blanket over something more real.

Beneath the grass, beneath the outermost mantle of rock, inside the smallest droplet, a world undistorted. Beneath all the reflections of something else, a place to grab hold. Something firm, as wanted by the eye.

Towards evening the hills turn blue.

Beneath the skin a body more real.

From under your hand I might slowly be revealed.

Albeit to your inverting gaze, or something—your eyes are like two pearls upon my hip.

To lie still and cower in the hedgerow.

Pain cannot be divided and cannot as such be understood.

There's no language for it.

In that way it is divine and yet a problem for music,

for art, and for people by and large.

To come back to a locked room that turns out to have been emptied during the night.

Or day.

The idea of *not* losing one's bearings.

That crucial moment. Some nails that are held in the hand and retain their coldness for a measure of time.

Different spans of time and the relation between them, the distance between two points.

To be of *general delight*.

It snowed, and the island became frozen into a sea that joined it to the mainland for months.

She told no one, but walked out into the white that lit up the woods from below.

The cover of snow speaks to the sky, as if together they possess some knowledge they continue to share, in that way to remain as one. A language requiring no translation, like a hedgerow connecting two places in the world.

January. Bells of frost beneath the horses' hooves, compact snow wedged to the iron shoe, the frog of the hoof blued and fraying in the freeze.

High walls balanced on the branches here.

It snowed, the way it had snowed for days, weeks soon.

Feet kicking up their fans of powdery snow with each step.

The darkness unrevealing of such detonations of crystal.

The crystal shares much with literature. Material held together in a particular pattern,

determined by particular rules. Structures repeating everywhere. He can see that, he says. It makes sense.

She remembers the snow consumed her tracks and that she was unable to find her way home again.

Trudging, then to pause and listen to the sound of her breath, which in turn startled her. No way forward, no way back.

Like a year suddenly past. Or just a summer.

She remembers she gave up and thought of a farewell scene, a parting from her family and lover. She recalls being surprised at who turned up in her mind.

How many were present, and the way the snow settled in her hair.

We come closer in a single seamless movement—a hand lifts the
long, dark hair of a girl aside in order that we may see her face.
A sick girl, draped over a toilet bowl, or a beautiful woman bent
over a bed—hair swept aside. It is with the slowness of the hand
that we approach the man's face.
We see the stubble of his beard.
No one has any use for a sick girlfriend.
No one wants a sick girlfriend.
His stubble is too prickly to be pressed against a face, is what we
think.
Visible millimetres beneath the surface of the skin.
His eyes are so dark.
He is despairing. We have no idea why, all we know is that this
is the case.
Despair at her condition, at the two of them, that it should come
to this, this point in the story.
Or at himself. It makes no difference.
Reproaches.
I don't want to go on, I can't,
I don't want to any more.
Who are you looking for.

The sounds she makes at the bar cabinet, on the tiles. She is standing still, but the sound of her feet crossing the tiles has been delayed by the image of him, the sound of his beard as it grows. Her hands passing over the bottles, not this one, not that one—as if there were a choice, as if it mattered.

Then the sound of her footsteps, and the sound of cognac sloshing inside the bottle. The two sounds combined.

And ice scooped into a glass.

What do we want with our bodies.

This perhaps:

to wake up again and have given them away, swapped them for something else.

Catastrophes, violent, near-sickening *reorganisations*, accidents.

She is tormented by the feeling of everything erasing itself.
The water, when almost gone from the tub.
Concentric rings, fungus spores on fruit.
White horses you have to follow.

You say you will not be destroyed here.

Or repeat some pattern that isn't even yours.

Or that you can't bear to see me imitate my mother any more, the whole time.

But then it's my mother who has taken over my body. Who puts herself behind your eyes, helping herself.

You fold our clothes to please me. You make an effort with something.

I am exempted.

I don't know who we are protecting by all this.

You, I suppose.

What is strong in the world is forever on its way to not being strong enough.

Termination everywhere.

The seasons phasing out.

That protest that exists in nature too; spring coming round again. The body's recollection of rhythm, the yearning for another state. I miss the repetition of you, mornings in a certain place, always, a certain way you had in sleep, at once troubled and unconscious. Standing behind you in the bathroom, seeing my body behind yours in the mirror. Or that twist of your body turning over on your side. As if you became stuck when lying in that position, as if the skin refused to let go. I imagine it will cease, and have already begun to miss it, though I am unsure what to make of it.

Cold feet fingers horses scraping at the frozen ground.

Everything ices up, and they're skating on the lakes. You not liking Berlin.

We travel to Boston together.

The cities we leave destroy us slightly. We've left a part of us in every place we've been.

The light comes in easier now, yet drains away from us so swiftly.

The things you have to leave behind.

Abandon.

The eye weeps for all it lost.

Cities no longer there. What are you supposed to do.

Before long the inshore waters will turn to ice.

I keep thinking everything's different now, firm ground beneath my feet; another, for the last time.

It all remains here within us, the lost is like a hollow chamber, a monument,

changeless as an echo, a grief that goes on *for ever*.

The only city that can endure is the city that crumbles.

The only firm ground that exists is the ground caving in.

And the loss and the grief are doubled as such,

and for all its luminous humanity it seems so very much *not* of this human fabric:

a withered lilac, one evening last week when I was home in Mols.

You can look at a withered lilac and feel convinced that from that moment on nothing more remains to be said about life and death.

Always losing something we love, something we are.

Again, we have lost what used to be, and yet are none the wiser for the loss,

the *lesson*.

None the wiser, nowhere near *changed*.

Still just a person, grieving over everything that can be remembered, a person *believing*, a person not living in the present world.

But then—

refusal. Not wanting to be a part.

On those conditions.

Autumn, simply, the vanishing of lilacs, the smell of soil after rain.

Firm ground beneath your feet;

the only firm ground that exists is the ground caving in; the only city that can endure is the city that crumbles.

Only it remains.

Nothing has changed, but everything is lost.

Not a single useful insight to be noddingly embraced, then worn like a shiny medal.

But still—the fragrance of the hawthorn,

the fatigued brown violet of the now definitively withered lilacs, field upon field.

An image, and another, and the two of us together,

wanting to share so much

before the inshore waters turn to ice, before the winter is *upon* us.

Between us.

The sun lays all things bare.

The fact of the wallpaper having come loose, and your skin no longer being the same.

Too much sun.

I love you, but I'm disappointed that—

I love you, and I'm disappointed that—

And you—

And us—

Maybe we could, maybe *I* could, be *here*.

With you.

Yes, you.

The characteristic restlessness of the voice.

You.

The stairs turn towards you.

Feet on this day, with no more snow.

But no more water in the rivers either.

Cities of quiet, slender women.

I never knew before that winter took so much away.

Or rather: takes.

You say you need to live in one place.

You emphasise *one* with a gesture, a downward cast of the hand.

I laugh out loud, because I've heard it before.

You stole it from me.

That knowledge. Or assumption.
Ashes to ashes, and so on.

They're burning off the fields.

It's against the law, that much at least she knows.

Everything unlikely collects together, a fireplace scene in which we gather in a knot of—

emotion.

Maybe the disappointment is hardest, the struggle to believe— and then no longer believe.

Nothing new being gained.

Nothing old being lost. Only the self again, nullified.

Whatever you used to be, it disappears, that's what it feels like, everything reduced to tiny, including the feeling of there perhaps being some meaning in all the madness.

The feeling of standing here on the corner where years ago we met, me in raptures at your sloppy appearance of which later I would so helplessly tire,

and later still miss doubly, to the power of two as it were, yearning to even feel something at all.

Apart from nostalgia, or reconciliation perhaps.

No longer being affected.

SAPPHIC FRAGMENTS

every single day

if not now

then you in the light
larger than any of us.

for you. Or your sake

all that beautiful glass
cupboards and drawers. What we have

more than either here or
we know.

after the war and the winter

who

the winter garden and I think I can live with that. Or the

after the war comes

and you really believed it?

winter again
          returned to them

impossible not to wait for you here. Do you think

scratching cement from between the stones

you brought and wanted me to

We divide everything into two equal piles

the flagline in the garden

help but believe me

freezing, I've just arrived

"dead"

The weather is fantastic, autumn is actually

and pulling down on the branches,   everything in
cold light.

and then I think,

no one

about to happen. For both of us.

joy and relief the first

But what I'm saying is
no party, so

throw myself out

I don't really know.

met. But for

Are you doing that too, walking on tiptoe

a year ago now

properly

talking and holding me tight at the same time

shovelling coal into your stove,

struggled to open the door

cold water and looking like wet

hadn't the courage and convinced myself that you knew.
current

the shore. Scrumping apples in Bogens recently

left me in the same state as

compassionate as

                                        otherwise

       winter, if not that, then

the sun is setting, the shadows are in some way more

.

of the treetops

and stitch by stitch, slowly

sedateness of the trees, becoming her slowly

as in the sea. That was the point she picked up the scissors

he said with a laugh
pity and envy in equal part,

shadows and golden light.

after all the trouble he'd caused us

sprouting on the beds of drained pools

as if we'd never

Your dreams are not your own, your skin
hands that

Warm bedrooms, the feeling of not needing

After our bath we lie like

never need

if you can make it so

if you think so

remains after the snow has melted.

count on it. You being there.

if.

like a formula for it

in the darkness as planets or snails,

them.

of things.

keep the different horses in different stables

not *here*.

it never happened

nice

all in one basket

OF DARKNESS

The setting sun. The way the light at first seems to dip down and coil, then launch forward to gild the landscape from a standing start, commencing at the far end of the fields where the hedgerow runs and the woods begin; gentle and yet enraged, like the seeming coldness of white-hot coals, or a seeming attention to matters of detail that is actually disappointment over some very basic states-of-affairs. The way things *fit together*, the way a passage of events draws something through the organism, summer autumn winter, the rhythm of the flesh, and the displacements that may also occur. The holding together of something, the hanging together by spite. A skilled carpenter whose box joints are made with such accuracy as to be quite as strong as the solid wood itself. The feeling of the sun and earth coming together in the same way as two people. The fact of not *understanding*. The body is the corset that keeps the thoughts in place; neglect the body and the thoughts withdraw, they seep away imperceptibly, the body undoing the ties, removing them from their metal eyelets; or the thoughts seeping away, tightening a frail drawstring in retreat, a string that eventually succumbs and breaks.

The girls stand on the riding ground with their horses. Seven girls and seven horses. The horses have been walked with slackened reins, now they lower their heads by turn, snorting muzzles in the dirt, a looseness of gait, the sounds they make. Nipping at grass. Flap, flap, muzzles flapping over tarnished teeth, the muscle of tongues, the rigid bristle of eyelashes seemingly inserted physically into the lids. They lead the horses around, stirrup irons flopped over saddles, drawn from the right, across the leather's gleaming seat, to dangle on the left, and likewise from left to right. The sun upon the black leather, a girl untangling a knotted mane, the thickness and stiffness of the hairs. A saddle scratched by a tack-room cat sharpening claws against the leather.

We see the horses with their riders, a girl and a horse connected by the reins. The horses led around the exercise ground. We watch the weary suppleness of their movements, the way seven pairs spread out over the pale oblong landscape. To all sides: fields extending like tongues, only a long, gravelled intestine cuts through their tossing contours, connecting the oblong with the stables; the manor farm at the end of the tree-lined track, the way it stands resplendent. A horse lifts a hoof, the elegant bend of the pastern, the elbow, the joining of the animal's various parts, the seamless movement from the joints, the stretch of the tendons, the contraction of muscle. Like planets, the horses disperse with their riders, their spreading out is the only movement in the frame, a symmetry to which one can only acquiesce. Some sounds— birdsong, farm machinery at work somewhere in the fields. A flaxen fringe swept from a moistened brow, a girth loosened three notches by a practised hand beneath the saddle flap, two girth straps at once and then the third. Quiet chatter that becomes particular by virtue of the sun's position in the sky. The movements of the horses, the body of their flesh, the spaces between them. The sun touches the horizon and ignites the fields. Lengthened beams of clutching red, the narrowest steel impacting on the eye.

At once the light is changed. A complete and simultaneous upheaval of all things, the sun powering its rays in every direction, as if they were arms thrown up in helpless surrender, only more vigorously, more elongated; the sudden coldness of everything, the emerging darkness that clutches at the girls, clutches at the horses, the painted oil drums and the striped poles, the helmet dropped in the grass.

Next, bodies are seen propelled, a few centimetres, twenty, fifty centimetres in the air, outstretched fingers, teeth bared and revealing of darkness.

An abrupt detonation.

Yet momentary, so brief as to be silence; and seconds later a turmoil of jetsam; the bodies of the girls, their open mouths and half-closed eyes. The wrench of the horses, a diagonal motion through the air, their long heads tossing back, seven forelocks unfurled like fans, a hock that nearly touches the ground, the outstretched forelegs, a tightened rein wrapped around a wrist. And then a sudden turnaround, as if everything has reached some saturation point, the apex of the upward thrust induced by the blast. The bodies of the girls then dashed to the ground, sprays of blood, festooning from a head or a stomach, trickling from noses and mouths; time altered, knees striking the earth, feet twisted awkwardly awry, a hand dragged through the air, or fanned out on the sandy earth. In this sudden downpour of death, an opening of the heavens, the bodies of the girls fall to the ground; and the hollow sigh of all things, the landscape, the arms of the sun drawing back like fingers retracting into a hand. A meltdown of day, and of the light.

Next, seven horses are seen, walking quietly about an illuminated oblong of ground in the midst of darkness. Eight floodlights are directed towards the area, their beams long and identical. The gait of the horses seems laboured and encumbered, as if they have traversed a very long distance through inhospitable terrain, searching for water or some other release. All unbroken expanses may be places for such release, perhaps even some kind of serenity. We realise a time has passed, that there is already a resignation about the wanderings of these animals. Around the enclosure, back and forth within the enclosure. Criss-crossed paths with spaces in between. The way the planets drag with them their moons, this is how the horses drag the cold frames of their girls. Reins wrapped tight around wrists, hands a blood-drained alabaster, fingers stiff and crooked as gnarled sticks of arthritis or hearts stricken with jealousy, racked and immobile, veins and arteries raised blue.

Of the night, much remains to be said. It is a task only for someone who can withstand the light, the glaring artificial light that floods the enclosure still. The horses go about their business; there is a flexing of joints, a casting of shadows. Of darkness, much remains to be said. Of the fields too, and the darkness of fields, their night. And of the horses, the horses of the night; of them, much may still be said. Moreover: the girls, the darkness that settles upon their alabaster skin, death so finely powdering the flesh, the green-white blush of death; the pale red of the lips.

She visits him again, for the first time in a while. They talk about that. He rocks gently, backwards and forwards in the chair. He's a good friend, she thinks to herself. He says he feels no need to fall in love again, that it is past now. After her, love is past. When he goes to the kitchen to get two oranges and some chocolate for their trip into the hills—before they realised they had no time to go to the hills, not that day—she noses around in his living room. The room is so very old. It's the first time she's been to see him. She passes her fingers across the spines of some books, the frame containing a photograph he took, and notices a bowl of withered fruit. Three peaches and an apple, their shrivelled skins, like dulled and sunken cheeks. She thinks it to be the saddest thing she has ever seen. Fruit, sapless and diminished, consigned to bowls of oblivion in the homes of abandoned people everywhere, broken people who yearn as yet, and who will continue to yearn in time to come, perhaps even forever—there, in such places, fruit is left, to decompose and slowly rot, though never quite to vanish. And there it remains, an organic timepiece measuring the hours from the first wrench of grief, when all things came to an end. It's as if these people wish to be reminded that everything has broken and come to a standstill; or else that life goes on, albeit *without them*.

And they themselves: the advanced age of the fruit becomes that of the body, its deterioration a correlate of their own organism. The grieving body and the dying fruit. The dying body's celebration of grief. Love becoming solicitude and a diligence as to *decay*.

Another friend's oranges, a Cox apple.

The mattress is on the bare floor, everything looks like it's fallen down; books piled all over, a table-top deposited without its legs, the shelving just five more or less horizontal lines between uneven rows of books. The sloping walls of the room cast shadows; the busy blade of the scissors. It's morning. Like the feathers of a wing, the books lean first one way then the other. Plants with their pots broken open like petals scattered on the floor, the white roots extending their pale and sleepy capillaries, soil spread about a core; like her heart, the core of her warmth and the occasional sounds that issue out into the room that encloses her body.

Her body, pumping warmth out into the room. It must be morning. You can tell from the light—soft, the way a body can be soft, an organic, fleshy light that does not stream into the room, but barges its way in, breaking things in its path, denting the thin partition walls, pressing the duvet flat as a frightened dog that cowers on the ground; the changing nature of the seams, from plunging indentations to these looser threads that strive towards the cotton like shallow water thrusting on to shore in windy weather, a shimmer of undulation in all things. She turns her head, though strenuously in the light, as if the light occupied the room like some thick transparent gel obstructing every movement.

The pillow retains the imprint of his head, the duvet cast aside, its corner turned down like the page of a book. As if to remind of something other than how far one has come, something more important that one (again) wishes to prevent oneself from forgetting, dismissing (once again) from the mind.

She mumbles a few words to herself. Her voice acts like everything else in the room: falling, then falling silent. His body, no longer there. Imprints of the human body are in some way more human than human bodies themselves. They contain the body as a negative, yet something more besides. A very fundamental voice, the tone of the human, that lingers, reverberating in the impression.

There's something satisfying about hearing a pop song's reiteration of a simple truth, for instance the banality of not knowing what you've got until it's gone. You lose someone, but at the same time gain a more complete picture of the love you nonetheless felt for that person. That's one way of putting it. But one might also consider that time changes everything; that the next day will always be new; that in a way it's too late to learn what you had to lose after you've already lost it—the glancing back over your shoulder, or the longer look, reveals the land you've covered to be different from the land in which you lived. The fields you left behind, the distance measured out in units of assumptions and kilometers. She stands with her hands on her midriff, concentrating on listening. But the light has the same effect as water, distorting all sounds. And yet she is certain, he is downstairs shaving with the electric shaver. The door is closed, she lies down and turns on her side. Lying there on the bed she can look down between the beams and see the door, which indeed is closed.

She gets to her feet. The pane is steamed up, a drop of condensation travels down the middle.

The sky is not blue but white; the light is the voice of the sun, unready as yet, though sleep-drenched it muscles in. The pane is soaking wet. She descends the loft ladder and cautiously opens the door of the bathroom.

He is facing away, quite apathetic.

She goes towards him. In the washbasin in front of him the electric shaver buzzes. He is standing quite still, staring out through the milk of punctured double glazing above the washbasin. She steps up slowly and pauses a few centimetres behind his back. He is naked. She turns her head, as if the light should take her photograph in silhouette, baring her cheek and glancing at her reflection in the mirror that is affixed to the wall next to the washbasin and which cunningly doubles the bathroom's size. Her face is partially obliterated. Only the part of it that is turned towards the light exists, the rest has collapsed, to dribble like thick glue from her hip, the eye left behind at the shoulder. She blinks, but only the left eye closes, the skin that surrounds the other, at her shoulder, contracts as if in resignation, a half-hearted smile. Great, black gloves cover his hands, his only garment. His eyes are different colours. In the mirror she sees the glint of something metallic. A few centimetres in front of his eyes, leaping sparkles of light as if from a Roman candle. But what she sees is a needle, threaded with thin red sewing thread. It protrudes from his eye. It was your brother, he says quietly. You were twelve. Is it still there.

He does not move, she does not reply.

The gloves are like an answer.

Can the past leave a person and come back for them again. The past, leaving you and coming back at inconvenient times.

His face is her face.

Their bodies have worked through the night, have lain in various positions, limbs draped like honey spun from the comb. Condensation trickles down the panes, both the windows are punctured. Through the glass one sees the sun upon the rooftops. Other planets are visible too, one is very near, dissected by the corner of the window frame. The planets drift as if suspended in water, close by and far away, sedately, prompting one to attribute their slowness to the distance at which they are seen, though in actual fact it is all about the eyes.

The eyes are planets too.

The slowness lies between the objects.

The individual body, the individual planet, possesses unimaginable speed and is proceeding insanely towards destruction. She reaches up and raises her eye to her lips. With two fingers she presses the orb between them. She stands for a moment, the eye in her mouth, the planet soon to block out the light from the window in front of them. One has the feeling of everything closing in, and yet one might easily claim the opposite. That would be true as well.

The outer wall, pale and yellow-washed. The cold stillness of the cobbled yard like a boiled sheet draped out to dry over a pile of sticks and left forgotten over the autumn and on into the winter, a face frozen in a kindly look, the coldness of demonstrations, symbols. They're winding the rectory up in its present form, selling it off to cut their losses. Everything's being marked up. A feeling of all the time that has passed, the struggle to keep things going, the realisation that it wasn't worth the effort. Sacrifices, losses. The two oak trees where the well used to be. Later, a leaf tumbling across the cobbles. Stepping under the trees one senses the trachea drop through the body; be dashed to the ground, thrust into the dirt and the tangle of roots, then a series of crippling blows that echo across the yard, causing the thin panes of the windows to rattle in their frames, the leaf to dry out and wither, turn brown, disintegrate and vanish, leaving only the frailest skeleton to be daubed against the yellow wall. The trachea is implanted in the ground like a fencepost; a fleshy paleness, blood as it drips from a half-open mouth, blood as it seeps, the trees that take on its colour, the roots becoming veins, the leaves then a deepening red, almost violet. The light in the yard transforms, now it penetrates the red cover of leaves. One cannot shout, one cannot hear, for this is a place of stillness. It comes with the soft yellow, one senses, the colour of the limewash. The trachea is implanted in the ground, the mouth is the eye of the well; there is a feeling of function and death.

The leaves no longer fall from the trees, not here, not anymore. The losses are inscribed in the stones and in the leaves, all that now becomes still here. Worse than the counting is the lull when no one is counting. Even he who was meant to count is lost.

The great hands of the trees bear witness.

As long as there is someone to count, to call something by name in a way that does not destroy; then there is something worthwhile, a rhythm in the world, a relation between two points.

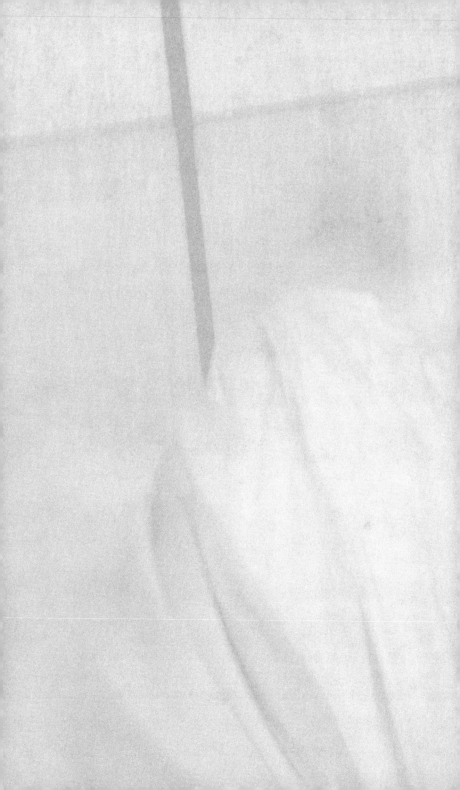

The sound of the glass, placed on the table.
A hollow sound, the glass encountering the surface,
amid this landscape of objects,
a hard sound of wood and glass, puddles and clouds,
oceans calm as millponds and the sun that glitters therein,
the water in the horse trough, the water in the basement,
the letters that float about, the scales of the fish as they reflect
the sun,
when the half-dead fish flap their tails,
twist their bodies and gasp on the quayside.
A fish-eye as it stares, without direction, seemingly at *everything*.
A gaze that has all the time in the world.
Why am I telling you this.
She says something along the lines of constantly missing someone.
    He can't really hear what she's saying, she speaks rather quietly
and there's the noise of the traffic too.
It's not because you don't love me, she asks.
He shakes his head. She seems changed, he thinks.
She closes the window—if we want to get out today we should
go now, before it's too late.
He nods.

A sack of rubbish dropping through the chute, a spinal column, green smoke rising from the oil drum in the back garden.

Maybe you should hold off writing something so harsh.

Until you know more about it.

Until you've felt what it's like *yourself*.

Whatever it is I'm supposed to feel.

Regret, guilt, gratitude for the love that

nevertheless still exists

for what

nevertheless once was.

I'm somewhere else completely, with no idea what I'm doing or

if I ever even knew you,

you say

you have learned such a lot from me.

The place where the shards of the urn were buried, at the foot of the tree, looks like a cathedral.

The sallow trunks turning dark against the light of the sky.

The sun entering in such oddly staggered fashion, a blade-box light, sword-beams of sharpened light penetrating the living body that time and again survives. The *character* of the light.

Light as it falls through windows high up in towers.

I almost miss the train, and had no time to put on underwear. I thought of the message it would have sent—if I'd missed the train. And you not being with me. How it could have been construed.

I like that place a lot, the whole idea of being scattered into the sea and the urn interred in such a cathedral of nature is beautiful.

The low fir trees. The tangle of brambles. You've said you'll come and pick brambles in September. I'll be in Rome then. The summer will be gone.

What has yet to happen is just as strong as what happened and went.

I'm pretty certain of what I would feel in this or that situation.

She looks back over her shoulder the whole time. She misses him now it's spring again: it comes back in loops, the yearning, with the same intensity, with the precision of the seasons, the *im*precision. She considers writing to tell you how it is. On a bad day he might come back in some guise. The idea of coming back for something you forgot. Not coming home, just back for something you're not exactly sure what is. Maybe then you could take it with you, in a little bag, carry it around with care or whatever, according to the circumstances. She sits out on the balcony. It's so quiet you could hear a man fold up a handkerchief.

All that cannot be transported, cannot be moved.

It's like moving a lake.

The body lagging behind thoughts that have gone on ahead,
the body always yearning.
This direction or that.

Forget it, she says in sleep.

The sunlight of morning reflects in the windows and is hurled back into nature.

The rear yard plunged into shadow for most of the day,
the underbellies of the horses,
the space between those underbellies and the grass, where e.g. the stream thrashes up,
when hooves kick through its water.

Smothered coals, a closed circle of sighs in the sand, their grey remains.

Everything the human body finds possible.

But we have no coals on which to walk.

New York, March 2012

Back pain due to misalignment of the pelvis. She did not have strong enough corset muscles to keep it in place when the irritation in the lower back began this fall.

42nd St/Bryant Park. *Soho Herbs and Acupuncture.*

I tear myself away like a boat from a quay at night.

You'll wake up early on such a morning and not have me there
to help you live, to get you through
the day, to allow you to breathe.

Breathe, he tells her. Drink.

It's so very common, they say, and she senses a calmness descend
upon them.

They walk over the bridges. The wind bites at her fingernails—cut
too short.

Animals graze, *regardless*.

The body's desire to get away with something.

The sun shines on the lawn, warming her lower legs; she walks
home through the cemetery.

You stop believing it will all go wrong,

and then:

you die.

When they came to the house they saw the trees were in leaf.

The winter, depositing everything;

the summer gathering something else up.

And you, where are you in all of this.

Some days in March, the fishermen put out to sea.

Inconsistencies.

Dead-end streets have no air.

Host and guest.

Some frozen tufts of couch grass.

Whether you want change or not.

You're not here.

Everyone agrees the situation is alarming.

In principle the garden should simply be plundered.

Summer pulls everything up by its roots, leaving plants, bushes, and flowers on the ground

like this

to wither.

Weeding the beds, at intervals.

Going to the zoo as if by ritual.

A particular way of descending into calm.

The distance between two objects may change by one object moving, the other object moving, both objects moving, or by some external force moving one, the other, or both.

Something with no obvious connection.

Is it a bad idea.

But love is no idea.

Quiet, quiet old song.

It's like my eyes are repeating something you're trying to put behind you.

As if I remind you of something you don't even know what is.

A body you can't forget, but more than that.

Josiah McElheny, *Modernity, Mirrored and Reflected Infinitely*, 2003. Mirrored brown glass, aluminium metal display, lighting, two-way mirror, glass, and mirror, 29 1/2 x 55 3/8 x 18 1/4 inches (74.9 x 140.7 x 46.4 cm).

Maybe he's just explaining something.

You know how the media work, you say. They want the drama.
Yes, I think, like you.
Sporadic movements forward, one knows them
far too well, the way one knows one's sisters
far too well.

Why do you always try to make me feel *worthless*.

That poster of the sunset that used to be on the wall outside the blue room upstairs.

Had it always been there, and if so who put it there.

Whenever it was.

At the dawn of time.

Counting down from ten and then starting from twenty.

The order of factors.

Ascription of value. *Value added*.

Every time I close my eyes I see the image of your back.

Apart from that I spend time looking at the view of the hills.

She thinks of an intuition she has,

the way it feels like she is stealing his love for her.

Borrowing isn't the right word.

Buying isn't either.

You look like you think we can protect him.

He's a child, he knows everything, he says proudly.

Are you going to drink any more of that, do you think it's a good idea.

Where are you, are you in here. Had an eye for that kind of thing, to be able to breathe.

It has been eaten up by silence, eaten up by stillness.

Your voice, I've forgotten what it can do.

Ground water and rain and blood and cries and spit. The beads
rattling across the teeth.
Him rising, shirt hugging skin
the way I did in the night, flogging another person as only I can.
As only you can.
Yearning in advance.

This afternoon's sun is yellower and heavier than the morning's; it's as if it needs to convince you the day is still here, is not yet gone, not yet; it is too early to surrender, spare me the white flags, for nothing in this world is too late. A dark-yellow sun, nourishing an almost maternal concern for everything that exists in nature—that which belongs there and also that left behind by people, a pair of sunglasses on a lounger, a glass, a paperback read by the wind at a speed one can only accept as a possibility.

The light turns blue.

The flagstones turn cold, a transition much like a sigh, something turning in on itself and vanishing. A balloon lasting a week at most. And the skin covering one's arms contracts in busy spasms, a window blind raised with a snap. The down of forearms rising, nipples hardening, breasts round as a rounded hand; if I lose my breath, the beat of my heart will present itself in a tremble of tissue, a shuddering breast. I sit down on the patio and look out. Even the sounds can be seen now. The sound of sand, a dry grinding that comes from light being so mean with its warmth.

We stand inside the woman's body and listen to his voice.

Hollow, his voice in the marrow and through the bone, the flesh, the skin.

Sound travels through water,

like a grain of sand or a shard of glass back out again, through the body,

a fish swimming against the current.

His shirt is wet, water settled on the field,

the stagnant pools, rain unable to escape,

through which they walk.

Clay soil—if we scraped all the mud from our boots it would make a land.

Or the sand whistling in the dry wind, settling in all folds, in the hair,

in the nostrils, in all notches and grooves,

all that sand together would make a land,

and not a single grain would be able to hide anywhere else again.

Run, he stresses,

we *ran* through the land.

I've forgotten how, that's all.

This is how we see him now, in the light of the descending sun, low and warm, behind him:

as if but muscle, overly tensed and quivering.

A man, getting to his feet, the mud that drips from his coat like entrails,

his nose, hands far too big,

the sun spreads between his fingers.

And the woman's eyes, suddenly they are the only thing in the frame: her eyes,

we see her smoke-blue eyes,

heavy lashes motionless, then the shutter of the lids, closing and opening over the orbs,

slicing everything in two. Everything you lost,

everything you never dreamed about.

We look into the woman's glassy eyes, but instead of seeing ourselves we see only the man.

The man, getting to his feet—

the man, again a body, parting the woman's gaze as

a knife through fruit,

and the beauty his broken body must now accept.

Recurring dreams.

What became of the crab apple tree,

the one we planted in the back garden.

Disease killed it, she says aloofly, unmoved, as if having assumed

nature's indifferent brutality, its indifferent

nurture of all things.

The dead, the living. A love of everything

in any form that might remind one of

indifference, but is the opposite: an attention to what there is.

In all new forms, in all the forms being may assume.

Forwards and backwards in time, the opposite of nostalgia, not

keeping anything for what it was,

but perhaps retaining something, or continuing to watch while

something dissolves,

so that something else might emerge in its place.

She considers it brutal, but at the same time rather elegant. She

says this out loud,

he nods.

In concentric rings originating from a central source, the disease

spreads through the garden.

And in concentric rings the creamy spores advance within the fruit.

She forms an eye with four fingers.

The sound made by his shoes as he crosses the floor.

The sounds are ominous—a rummaging, rustling upheaval of his very being, like a clawing rake catching on a lower branch of the hedgerow, snagging in a tangle of brambles; a gashing of bark, sweat that starts to trickle, leaves crushed and crumpled. Looking down into the apartment from above is like peering into a shoebox furnished by a child, with tiny chairs and tables and rugs.

He is lying with his ear against the wall.

She paints her nails in the next room. He hears the drip of varnish onto the surface of nail, hears its application, counts each and every brush stroke. We view the two rooms as chambers of the heart, looking down from above.

All walls are thin, all sounds clear to him, and he is sharp, she thinks to herself. He can cut through a matter, grasp what things are about. Individual sounds, their *significance*. He knows everything, he sees it all *from above*.

Her glossy nails reflect the bulb of the blue halogen lamp. He hears all of this, and what she *imagines* too; what she *plans*.

To gaze at a glassy object and see the world reflected there without oneself being a part of that reflection; in that way to cease to exist as anything but the gaze of an eye; and yet to be that very gaze; a most peerless feeling indeed. The opposite of coming to a new and desolate town and seeing oneself in everything.

It may be the case that one comes to a new town, desolate and acutely visible to one's own gaze; that one seeks refuge in a place where such an image exists in which to vanish; or that one finds a particular book and reads a poem, or simply the remains of a poem, and that one in that way vanishes, to become but a gaze.

The sun draws the colour from all things.

I remember thinking this and being assailed by the feeling of it being obviously correct. That this really was the way of things; the sunlight as a drain. Now I despair at ever having entertained the thought, how I ever could have felt that way, certain of something. One could also assume that light fills the world with colour. It would seem just as obvious, and today just as correct.

What then to trust.

What do we have other than the days, and in addition to them a gaze that on occasion might see. There are cracks and crevices, even in the laws of nature there are cracks and crevices; and there is light, entering and departing all things.

I don't know if a person can take leave of something; I don't know how it would help. I know that you are here, that you are here still.

The following day, on the instruction of her betrothed, the men came to drag Lucia away to a brothel; but the young woman stood firm as a mountain. They brought axes and roped her at the belly and knees. Still she stood firm. She bit her lip, her jowels trembled, and yet she stood firm as a deeply rooted tree, a mountain almost.

Stood.

Their axes were useless, the men conceded, wiping the sweat from their eyes with curses. Presently they came with firewood by which to burn her at the stake, but once again their efforts were in vain. A number of the strongest men then approached to bend her head backwards and she did not resist. The men put tongs to her gleaming eyes and wrenched them out with resolve, though not without several being compelled to vomit, their backs turned, the sound of a snapping branch, the sigh of bark under the blade surprised them perhaps. Or else she stood firm and gouged out her own eyes that no man ever again might desire them. Often, she is depicted with her eyes on a tray or in a small bowl. Or as here: on the stem of a flower held in her hand. She looks down at her eyes; there are six eyes in all: those on the stem; those in her sockets, by which she sees; and our own, in this instance mine, the two eyes I am forever lending out. One can pray to her, for she is

Saint Lucy, the patron saint of the blind. No one else may desire them ever again. Such a thought.

There's always someone who is parent to another. I have become mother to my mother. She phones again and I am gripped by a feeling of solicitude I imagine must be the same as a mother's solicitude for her child. A recurrent feeling of her not being able to look after herself, me having to be there more often.

Different things being placed in small bowls. Beads in a bowl. Grain. Some colourful candy and raw red meat with a white marbling of fat. It's as if the sounds trail on. The images are more sound than image.

The high panelling, the three bright rooms facing out towards the mouth of the harbour; the storm and the rain lashing the trees, no one ventures out today. The siren sounds; you say we're safe here, we're safe here. The rising water is cause for concern, the canal swelling still, and they listen to the radio as it rains.

They have been cooped up indoors for some time now; they have begun to mark off the days on the wall by the door—one mark for each day, the fifth diagonal. It was amusing to begin with, a kind of joke, but now it's different. They try not to look when they pass through the hall on their way to and from the kitchen. The balcony is under water, the plants have lain down in their pots and troughs, and three scrawny pigeons have set up camp there, looking ever more wretched in their sorry plumage. Their eyes have dulled and become milky, in contrast to the glassy surface of the water that is disturbed only by the rippling eyes that are made by raindrops. The choppy waters of the canal rise up under the bridge, fat liquid slabs pressed up between the slats, sheets of spray and salt. She awakens slowly on the sofa, has dreamt, something about her sister, her sister being angry with her and shoving her backwards, causing her to fall. In the dream she decided to punish her sister, and pretended her fall to be serious. She lay there on the floor, as if she were unconscious. From the darkness behind her eyelids she watched as her sister fell silent and became gripped by fear, then to run away and fetch some men who lifted her up; that's her lying there, be careful with her. And they took her to the hospital, where the doctors had to operate right away. They shaved her skull, and she knew as she lay there that she would have to let them operate on her brain even though there was nothing wrong with her—she knew she had to go through with it. She sensed her sister's distress and deep regret, the way it mingled with her own, and yet all the time she felt that little dash of pleasure at seeing justice to be done. Having to pay for one's sins. The meting out of punishment.

She lies with the old white throw covering her, the one they can't discard even though it's worn thin and frayed. Light falls through the clouds. Razor-finned spheres fly through the air, slashing their way through everything, furniture, bodies—you're bathed in sweat, you've been dreaming, he says. He grips her and lifts her head as if she were an infant or the victim of some accident, a casualty. He pulls her up towards him, kissing her on the mouth, as if a kiss in some way counted in his favour. She is limp with sleep, the sleep that courses through her body. She is draped over his shoulder and stares out through the windows, out across the sea, another Venice entirely now; and the sheets of salt water thrusting up from under the bridge are a glassy arcade, ten thousand mirrors, the city rebuilt here in the midst of its demise. The harsh facades of the new buildings on the other side of the canal. No one ventures out, a single face in a window, but that was earlier. Not many windows can be opened anymore, no one left with cigarettes to smoke and windows to open in order to do so, and the last of the daredevils who took to the waters for a swim have either vanished or given up. He took hold of her knee and lifted her leg over the edge of the sofa, pushed her beneath him. The sea is rising, swallowing the bridge, suffocating the columns, its waves unfolding across the harbour area, the cobbles, consuming the old wooden sleepers, the tables, flooding the lawn, dissolving the trampled-down turf, thinning the soil that now begins to float, little scraps of bark and tiny stones filtered through the blades that stand like bristles, wave like bristles beneath the water, the calm beneath the surface, the rush of the waves drawing back, the grass bending with the movement, mimicking, then upright again; the next wave, and the next, and another. The sky contracts and tightens, different strata of cloud separating in bands, revealing something white beyond, light from somewhere, only then it is gone, fading away into grey. Where they are most compact, these grey ribbons shaft towards the ground in dark violet, a negative light, darkness decimating all things before it, sealing the view from the windows of this apartment. Everything closes in on them, the occasional chinks of brightness in the clouds are passages opened to allow something through. Metallic curtains of purple-grey rain. They exist inside this cubicle. An impending light, approaching like a calendar date or a saturation point; reactions, implosions, matter expanding and contracting. His back is turned and he cannot look into her eyes; if he looked at her now, he would see what was behind him reflected, but he looks at the wall, the splendid high panelling, the door leading out.

Who is most hopeless. Who is most in need of drawing on some
addiction, drawing on the other.

A boat torn from its moorings in the storm, the darkness of the prow; the darkness that lingers about the beds and bodies, the hands folded and slid beneath the pillow, or the hands that hold another body, the cheek pressed against the throat of the other, the warmth between the two bodies; seaweed caught and then extracted like her hair as she drowsily opens the catch in the bedroom and the wind wrenches the entire window from her hand with a bang, like a sudden wound, or a garment of leather ripped open at the seam; horse riders tumbling like hail from the sky.

The wind breaks up the landscape in a raging clamour of lashing branches and rattling gates, bringing moisture to the eyes, sweeping across the open expanse between the boundary and the fringe of the woods, scraping and clattering over the frozen earth, over the tops and stubble. Winter lasts longer than summer because it reaches so far inside of everything. It counts and appropriates the ribs. It heaves the branches apart and hurls them together again. Time is bound in the movement, and winter paws and claws with its frost and its storms, ceaselessly altering the form of all things; frost and thaw and frost again, the same coat buttoned many times each day, done up and undone, sweaters and scarves drawn around the body, wrapping it up, the body flapping its arms to keep warm, or stamping the snow from its boots. A young man battles to light up a cigarette as winter batters the trees. A new layer of calcium with each passing day. Stargazer, horses chewing the bit, heads tossing back, the urge to move on in any direction, movement being enough; every street corner awaits a presence, shaped to accommodate anyone who lingers.

She could wake up to a mass of people staring in at the window; in the cold, their faces would be unclear, the pane steamed up by so much breath; a droplet of moisture could travel down and expose a section of chin, collarbone, or chest.

She often had to remind herself that nature possessed no will, that as such it was *impersonal*—unwanting of human contact, not meaning anything by snow. Unbelieving. The snow, glittering. The sea, glittering. The veins of her forehead are made conspicuous by frost, and she has noted that the long, almost invisible scar on her brow from the time she rode a horse under a low tree seems to emerge more clearly in the whiteness of such light. She takes off her gloves and holds them between her knees, feeling her brow with the tips of her fingers.

There's nothing to feel.

The snow is dry.

The sounds are quick.

To sit and linger behind a stack of firewood and stand up as the horses come galloping by; they leap in the air and swerve away; fear creates empty spaces around that which is feared; the strange patterns of alarm, deposits of empty pockets of air incalculable as sea currents, plunging falls and hours spent alone, the body being unable to find a hold, connect itself. A lightbulb hanging from its socket on the ceiling. Getting up on one's own to boil an egg, picking away its shell and running a hand over one's arm. The dream of a summer cabin or a lighthouse.

Is the sun the same as the eye. Is sun.

To walk to the other end of the town, to the lock, like peeling a fruit and standing with something very bright in one's hand.

An arrangment.

It is the height of summer and they are all together at last. The women and girls are standing in a row in the driveway, all five lined up between the two pillars. The men are at the sides, three on the right, three on the left. And then—this being the whole idea of the photo—on top of the two pillars that serve to mark the entrance of the driveway, the two tallest of the men stand holding each end of a long branch. From a distance it looks almost like a roof they are holding up above the females' heads, or at least a canopy of some kind. The effect is that of a rectangular frame— the lower edge formed by the heads, the upper edge being the outstretched arms and the branch they hold between them, the sides are the pillars and the straight figures of the two tall men. The intended motif is thereby the field behind them, the photographer being positioned at the house rather than the road, as one might have expected. The rectangle frames the landscape and becomes as such an institution. A sorry mulberry bush steals the beholder's attention and becomes the picture's true subject, perhaps along with the dial of a watch worn by one of the men, which gleams in the sun. It, too, calls for attention.

All the females have dark hair and are wearing dresses with

waistbands, though this is merely a part of the frame. In another photo—a family portrait—a sheep has found its way into the picture. It stands there, white as white with bulging eyes, yet there is nothing about such an animal that can disturb the image, no style of dress to signpost an era and thereby beguile the beholder. It is as if people who really *feel* things, their faces—the way they can make time burst open like ripened fruit out of which seeps the clearest liquid, a sense of our being *here*.

She is woken by him gripping her arm. *You are innocent when you dream, live and let die, get yourself out on the ground, boys don't cry.* Though he is the one running a temperature (40.2 degrees), it is she who feels hottest. Her breathing. She gasps for air. Dogs running out in front of cars, running away on crushed legs. A black metal anchor had embedded itself in the skull. It was a miracle in a way, that the boy wasn't dead.

She looks at the painting of the track in the woods. It's winter, the snow is blue in the shadows of the fir trees, yellow in the clearing further ahead. Stacks of firewood line the track, stockpiled like bundles of banknotes, a speech scribbled on a napkin and stuffed into a pocket for later use. A defence of some kind; a man comes walking as if on his way through the painting and out of it, and yet he is coming towards us, towards where we are in the picture.

To huddle together when all is calm and peaceful, the longest of days.

To step on one's own toes.

The war passed like a sickness, I am always the same. Never any progression as such. Life runs the other way inside her, and thus she moves. Something inside her.

The sun is low in the sky, the way the moon was.

The wall is stuck to the picture like a playing card under a cup raised to the lips. The sky sticks to the eyes. Russia looks far too big on such a map. Too much of one thing. More than can be coped with. She runs her fingers over the painting. She cuts herself on the hole. Though no shard can be seen, she cuts herself. Blood trickles down her finger, drips to the floor in highly complex rhythm, a very poor kind of rain, a few drops is all. The sky collapses into the clouds, making them dark and heavy.

We go to church at Christmas, and he comes with us. Next year—
this is what he says—we are going to spend Christmas with his
family. In the USA, where they live. They sit there on the plane.
She happens to suggest it might not be that important for them
to go over every other year. His family being so easy and relaxed;
your family being the way they are.

He says nothing for a while.

Maybe she thinks, now that his father's dead and his mother
moved away, and his brother moved away—maybe I think he
doesn't have that kind of dream inside him anymore. He holds
up his hand when they come to serve the food. She feels she has
to do likewise.

For his sake.

Maybe at some point tell him she thinks she might stay.

An experiment using iron filings on a sheet of paper. She remembers moving the magnet underneath the paper, the patterns it made.

Adults fall asleep when they come home to visit their parents. Not because they relax, but because so much time must pass through their minds.

The very soul of France, don't you agree, he says. She doesn't know what he's talking about, it could be a musician, a dish, or a cookbook.

When she came up to the house her hair was almost dry, or at least it hung down in strips, dark marrow encased in a dull, yet lighter crust of frazzled strands. She had no clothes on, only a towel wrapped around her.

She hadn't seen him.

He'd left the car up at the road and walked.

The winter crop upholsters the fields from below, a dusting of green velvet or cotton, growing and encasing the soil; a mantle made visible by the storm, the wind's shawl of snow, gusts blowing open the coat, wrenching away the shawl; the snow as it drifts and piles, and then these islands of green. This green that wants to *witness*. This *merciful* green. Whatever mercy could be—a hand held out beneath you, perhaps, or a whole body protecting another. A colour. Sun. To describe an image to someone may be a kind of love. The green beneath the snow bears some semblance, but is not. It's nature, that's all. Nothing to depend on, and as such there is some coincidence yet. Points of similarity. The distance between things and us. That which survives another day, and that which is lost.

Other women say we look like each other; our boyfriends say we're night and day. I'm night, I think to myself, though I can see the opposite could easily be said—I'm the one with fair hair.

I'm sitting on the floor in the living room, it's my mother's birth-day. We've all come home. We're going skating, only no one's got skates. Or rather, we think there might be a moving box with skates in it in the loft, but they must have been there ten years, more than likely they're right at the back now and can't be got at. It would be too much trouble. Only later, on the ferry back to Sjælland, does the thought occur to me that they would have been too small, children's skates.

I find it odd no one thought of it, or said anything.

My boyfriend is sitting on the floor too, we're watching a film from what my mother calls the old days. Our cheeks are red from being out in the cold on the pond. They sweep the snow away with a machine that looks like the kind of cultivator we use to dig up the vegetable garden in the spring. It's got brushes instead. They start at the edge, moving along the shore, tracing the oval of the pond, this dark rink of frozen water. The water, darker than the snow. Two separate rectangles have been cleared, on one of which they're skating and playing ice hockey now. Some of the kids from Egens Havhuse. Between the two rectangles is a snaking path. My boyfriend goes over and studies the work—the man is clearing a circle but has started from the outside, the machine keeps throwing the snow back inside the circle. He's going to end up with a pile in the middle. It won't take much wind for all his work to be in vain. Do they always do it like this. He stands with his gloved hands in his pockets.

There are so many layers in the landscape, the solemn trees closest to us cut up the picture like the cracks of an oil painting, a fracture in the wall in the corner of the bedroom. Is it worsening. It's hard to tell from day to day. A translation—then, now. The past, continually collapsing like buildings behind us, becoming something else.

They have driven through the woods to the beach so they can watch the bonfire. There is no other way to get it said than this, the hard way. They have come to see the bonfire, so no one says anything until they reach the car park outside the beach hotel.

Her mother turns off the ignition and they sit for a moment in their coats, a dampness in the interior and under their clothes. They're wearing lightweight summer coats, their skin is tanned and their hair bleached by the sun: it is the height of summer. She and her sisters, her mother, her father. They can see the bonfire from the car, but no people. It feels odd, the bonfire piled up like a peak on the empty beach in the rain—the summer of 2004 is a summer of rain. Up at the hotel the grey flagline slaps against the pole, beating out a weary rhythm familiar from the harbour almost any day in spring when boats are made ready.

Curtains of rain across the sea.

A man trudges past, a dogged angle in the wind. The car ticks. The air is not cold, more close and blustery at the same time. Her younger sister unclicks her seat belt. They are startled by the sound as the belt retracts, the metal clasp striking the window.

The unobtrusive sea, its waves are an unsettled band of greyish brown. The light is not the summer's. Her sister shuts the car door behind her, they all get out and stand for a moment gazing in their different directions: their mother looks towards the woods, her sisters consider opposite ends of the sea; she stares blankly at the sand. There are candles in all the windows—it's too dark for Midsummer's Eve. There's something unnatural that doesn't fit in with the season, the time of day. At the water's edge she veers off and follows the shore like a sphere rolling through the groove of a wooden board. Seen from above it looks like the shore and all its sand empty out into the sea; the undulation of waves, repeated extensions of green and white, fanning out as they break; the effervescent rush before retreat. The sound of—a sphere in wood, a very simple sound against the murmur of the sea, always the same—whether heard or not, it exists. The bonfire won't be lit, her mother says definitively.

They are quiet.

They stand with their backs against the car, then walk past the boathouse, where the lifeboats are stabled, and down through the dunes. Her sister picks up a branch blown from the bonfire to lie like a bone in the sand. She tosses it back onto the pile, that reacts with a groan, the slightest of landslides, a few smaller elements rattling down a level or two, like a body turning in sleep when touched by a hand.

They walk around the bonfire, considering it from various angles, though all the time from below and all the time with distrust or a feeling that something is wrong with it. Once they've been all the way round, they stop.

He's got things in jeopardy: money, and his face.

The garden is an eye, the lawn swathed in rippling green; and in the middle are the perennials, older than us all. You amble around them, casually, as if you were a planet fastened to its orbit around the sun, older than us all; or else you are a cone of light in search of something, a pencil beam penetrating the eye in order to find some weakness, or perhaps even disease. The light has no age. Light is no older or younger than the eye on which it falls. You stop and jab a finger at a plant. They're strangling each other, you tell me softly. A bed like this is war; the minute you look away, it's war.

You nod as you speak. I can see the way your neck bends and extends, the silhouette of your head, your fair hair that in the light of afternoon looks like a cluster of aquatic plants. It's a shame, you say softly.

I have always thought you to be a child, but now I see that you are not. You have all ages in you, while I stand here bare, a tableau like the perennials. No age or time will ever latch on to me, and thus I am already someone you miss.

I am barefoot in the grass, walking backwards now out of the garden. I hear you speak to me. I see your girlfriend at the kitchen window, preparing pigeons and curly kale with a face that seems new every day. Unlike us, your girlfriend masters the art of living.

She lives the same way as fledgling birds—they hatch out in a nest, oblivious to all that exists outside, and die if they fall from the nest too soon. I have dreamt about being like her—of being her—but today I am no longer sure what kind of dream that is, or whose. Some of us draw the strangest of straws—within us collect all the stray dreams that exist in the world, those left over. It becomes impossible to tell the difference, which are one's own and which come from without and belong to another. The lawn is alive with caterpillars, it makes me itch, and you let me off the hook. Gone, I feel the same as I do in the garden and when I am with you—completely alone. And thus we squeeze the juices onto our brows, until we no longer can remain inside the body, until we are beasts that cause the stomach to turn, or perhaps until the human being within surrenders with a wince. You think I am still close by, but you could turn around at any time and see something else. I slam shut my eyes as I leave—the metallic clatter of the gate, before everything once more is still.

A length of knitting relieved of its needles on account of alcohol. A number of stitches waiting to be unravelled. A kind of vulnerability that is almost nauseating to watch—fingernails on a blackboard, that kind of nausea, that instead of rising up inside engulfs a person from below, the kind that cuts one's consciousness into very thin slices and serves them to a father who leans forward across the table and holds forth on the matter like a schoolteacher explaining something about which he has only the slightest knowledge, or a businessman on the verge of closing a profitable deal, with the utmost stringency, a recipe or a set of rules a person can pass on or teach, exercises to strengthen the small of the back, studies indicate, etc. Stains on a shirt. Various substances.

Maybe the problem isn't so much *hoping* for something else.

He lights a cigarette and the palm of his hand is illuminated like the inside of a cave.

A drop of moisture released from a branch. Autumn: leaves descending like tired faces in the streets.

Steam drawn out of the window. Rising.

You're paranoid. She reaches for the red wine and empties the bottle into her lap, leaning back against the counter.

What are you doing, he asks calmly.

Having a miscarriage.

Okay, he says with a nod.

He drinks from his glass. That's all we've got, he says, pointing with it.

The light of summer draws the colours from the world.

Green and blue. No matter.

The dismal belly of the hedge, the leaves of the birch though brightest green, waving in the breeze, whenever there is one; limp as droplets when there is none.

Clustered weary on the branches, those thin arms.

The birch.

Birch trees, wandering, as if troubled.

Troubled by e.g. war, or the promise of death.

Was it so bad you thought you'd die.

So bad the only thing you want is to die.

The next image is from Normandy, the coast there. No people, just an empty beach. Waves. Nothing but waves and the sound of waves. The sound of the garden and the sea.

Presumably, he wants to see you happy.

He knows I won't be. He knows I never will. He's not that stupid.

He knows me.

I got this idea about you and that lump of amber, like it was the amber that picked you up. From the beach.

Thus march the trees in a flicked-out fan from the garden, now from the sea: like soldiers to the land, over the beaches, slowly to the house as if risen up from the ocean itself, kelp about their ankles, seaweed for hair, barnacles beneath their soles, calves encrusted, occasional mussels embedded in algae, entwined around the thighs.

Like the sun.

Returning to a lodger who will turn out to be gone. Washed away. Nothing here, whatever happened to …

And in reply, a pair of shoes, or perhaps only a single shoe. Left behind before a house taken by the swell, laces rotting.

He bent down and picked up a lump of amber, tapped it cautiously against his teeth and held it up to the light.

Come closer, he said. Look, he said. And as the trees withdrew, they shone through all things with their white bark, and beams of light were their gaze.

We look into the woman's glassy eyes, but instead of seeing ourselves we see only the man.

The fact of our not seeing ourselves in the woman's gaze.

The exchangeable nature of love, and always: promises of the opposite.

Approximately eighty per cent of what may be said about me may also be said about you.

To circle a building by allowing the index finger to follow a mortar joint in the brickwork. Freedom is something one used to have, found only subsequently and in hindsight, and thereby such a nostalgic idea, and exactly that—an idea.

The darkness of the woods, *regardless*.

Like your face during that time. Some favours I do for you, without you really noticing.

Look what you've done.

The sun adds and subtracts indefinitely, like an abacus in the play area on board the ferry, first one side, then the other; you get up early and say you want to get something done today. When later we walk around the lake we must clamber over fallen trees. Or rather, you bypass them, holding down thin branches from the top of the crown with your hand. The oak trees had just come into leaf before being cut down, the way a person might think of something they should remember to say. Summer, and a conversation that could have been.

I keep thinking about the way I banish the sickness to a place outside of me by calling it some particular name. This or that. I don't know if you could call it a breakthrough, I don't really believe in stuff like that. Maybe the speed can be adjusted, but the crash is always going to be inevitable. Maybe the rate at which a person disintegrates can be slowed down—maybe that's what these fleeting realisations can do. I survive by the language. The language as an additional body part, a substitute heart for when the other one stops, an extra pair of lungs. Salvation, to possess a voice. Two kidneys.

And what if it is not dreams and the night that disrupt everything, but the day that makes everything contract and shrink. Like when the moon looks bigger when you're close to the horizon. What are the proportions, what perspective is right.

You marched through the city, dressed in black, red flowers in women's hands, and hooded. As if hoods or colour could ever keep something so fluid together, knots and ties. A dog tags along. The boat waits at the headland, at the jetty, engine chugging. You step on board one by one, like a necklace of beads stretched between two hands, the gap of elastic thereby exposed, one bead at a time allowed to pass. One sees a foot, and then another, the footwear, stockings. Nylon, leather, stripes. Bright-coloured shoes are comical, in a heart-rending kind of way.

Unexpected guests in the middle of another of our arguments.

You know how it is. If anyone came through the door now you could force a smile. *Gerbera*, I think they were. I think they were gerbera, the flower heads they scattered on the sea, bobbing on the swell.

Strong colours.

The stars seen from Earth are more numerous than all the grains of sand in the world. The photograph's distortion of the subject, the ends of the horizon curving like the corners of a mouth. To make the aperture big enough to let in all light; to pluck the flesh from the pigeons; to part a crown of the darkest hair.

Where do you imagine the money's going to come from.

They have reached all the way around, emerging now into

the clearing and walking the final stretch towards us. We can hear them talking, they have been hidden from us by trees and the boathouse on the other side. The denser the foliage, the less intimate became their talk. Whatever a person endures, it leaves a mark in their language, the way the sky determines the colours of the sea, children always being the children of their parents. My mother is unhappy about the little blue tattoos they made on her breasts before commencing the radiation therapy. They look like dots made with a ballpen—they'll fade in time, she says to comfort me. A pile of timber darkens at the shore; shreds of fibre torn loose like hair floating in water, hair blowing in the wind. A softness in the language, and in her face.

Is it possible to reflect and be happy at the same time.

She stoops and draws an arm of the beech away from her face. The sunlight cleaves the trunks, the trees subside into the forest floor. He stumbles and nearly falls. The path is studded with rocks, like bald heads breaking the surface, a thousand metres from the burial mound. There are paths below the ground and everything is continually in the process of becoming something else. You regain your footing and reappear at my side. I found an A4-size envelope today, on the front of which my mother had written: *To be opened in the event of a new winter coat. Love, Mum.* I opened it—the adhesive glittered blue—and put the three thousand-kroner notes it contained in my wallet, the envelope in a black box I keep by the DVD player and your records. I had already bought a winter coat. I felt glad I hadn't opened the envelope before and spent the money on something else, like food, or just frittered it away. In fact, I thought I had.

They burned off the fields, the smoke was purple and settled on the landscape like a dusty cloak. The risks of mistaking loneliness for something other than loneliness are various. When you lie on your back, a shadow makes your nose look squint. I don't know if I believe in optical illusion. Or if there is anything else.

Whatever can be said about reading poems can also be said about living or being in a relationship. A number of requirements, or instructions given.

Your toes inside your sandals, nails colored black.

It's all like looking at a 3D image—to make it work you've got to concentrate on a point beyond the screen.

I've noticed I feel happiest owing you something. Having something to return, being one favour behind.

During our first months together you got rid of various items of sentimental value, things that concerned your relationships with other women before me—letters, handcuffs, jewellery, lotion. We too have accumulated stuff, I see, and now I wonder if I could become a collection of remnants in the same way.

We are back at the clearing where we started. Our towels lie brightly at the bench. Beyond the trees, the burnt-off fields moved like an ocean, a gentle swell of smoke, ever sinking, never retreating. No higher bid.

My cousin is drinking himself to death. That's what we do in my family. Some of us, anyway. It's a slow way to die and belongs to the indecisive, those who can actually see there might be something worth living for: the beauty that exists in the world, and love—the chance of fondness, still. My other cousin writes to me on Facebook and says it looks like he's on his way out, that it's a battle now. I write back and tell her I thought he was getting better the last time I saw him. The time we visited. I even thought he'd come to some realisations. Or one, at least. She tells me his condition has not deteriorated, but that he's been more dead than alive for a long time, that his internal organs have been steeping for years.

My family has lost several in that war. My cousin tells me she's developed her own strategy. It's a question of being unsentimental, she writes. Let them drink themselves into the grave if that's what they want, as long as they accept it's their own choice—and if they happen to decide something else one day, then all well and good. Let them know you're there for them if needed; but you can't spend your life urging and appealing, begging and pleading, and always getting let down.

My mother is cut up about something I wrote. She feels like she's being held up to ridicule all the time. I suppose it's the surrendering of power. The child claiming the right to her own story. Sharing it with others, if that's what she wants. A miniscule fragment of the self that can be handed out to whoever; like a garden in autumn, with always a leaf releasing; or a body soaking in a tub, beginning to dissolve, tiny cells of skin, or flakes, floating like a film on the surface of the water. She says she finds it hard that I always make her a *victim*. It's an odd thing to say, as if it short-circuits the brain or leaves it in a state of self-fuelling oscillation. Who makes who a victim. When I was fourteen I put a newspaper clipping up on the fridge with a round, red magnet. There was a picture of a woman writer who wrote about the conflict in the Middle East. It had to do with the role of victim, the way it made the bloodshed possible. Because the victim can always do as he likes. The same applies to kindergarten. Who makes who a victim, who is comforted. The greatest revenge is perhaps simply not to be there any more. But when you're waging war a hundred kilometres apart and are there no longer, you have never been closer. Maybe that's how it is too. The more you fight, the closer you become; the more space you take up being missed, as an imprint, the closer you are.

Dear cousin,

A brief word from me here in Nørrebro, Copenhagen. It's a cold day, the fourteenth of February. I'm sitting here trying to work on my new book and happened to think about you. As I've done often of late—hearing how you are from your sister and my dad and wishing the very best for you. Hoping you're getting better. Are you able to eat? Is the hospital food any good? For someone who knows as much about food as you do it must be a trial sometimes to find the appetite to eat and get well, that must be hard enough on its own.

It's been a while now since we spoke. I live here on Fælledvej in Nørrebro with my boyfriend. You haven't met him yet. Who is it now, I hear you ask, and I can understand why. There's been quite a few the last couple of years. A coming and going of men. I can't manage being on my own. Still, this time I think it's going to work out. Nine months already, which is something.

I think about how many ways I can tell a lie and that I'm good at it.

I'm rewriting my essay. Revising and making amendments to keep my family happy. I'm manipulating. The story about that letter to my maternal grandmother, the way it got photocopied and put away. A simple matter of retaining something, now an issue about having the right to tell. They say history belongs to the victorious; but I am no victor. I have violated something in which I truly believe. And acquiesce so as not to be shunned.

I walked around the city lakes yesterday so I could talk to her. After a week it could no longer be postponed.

The energy my sisters get out of it.

It was nearly dark as I went. Darkness falls early on this land in winter. It surprises me still, how early. It creeps up and assails you. We talked about my father, how impossible he is on vacations. There's so much resistance in him—fear, I think to myself, that maybe has to do with alcohol in some way. His childhood, with a father who drank, drank and wrote the whole time. I think his own take would be that it was down to some other stuff—his mother, no doubt.

In a way, the whole thing is a tragedy no matter which way you look at it, whatever the truth of it. The way something can be *handed down*. My mother and I—it's not hard to see we're in it together when it comes to him. Enemies, loved ones, frost, winter. Nothing binds together like that.

The seeming potential of alcohol with regard to cementing kinship. Or maybe just that exactly—kinship. The frailty of family, the darkness of it.

A few days later I'm on the phone to my best friend. We talk about my mother and the essay. He says it's the crux of the piece—that it's extremely important to retain, my reflections on wanting to preserve memories and who owns the past. He thinks I've brought it out well in the writing. I tell him about the feeling I get having those talks with her. Like being put in your parents' car and made to visit some aunt and uncle you don't like. We laugh about that. I go back to the office, balancing my tea.

I read somewhere that men don't want to hear about their partner's previous erotic experiences. That it just ruins everything. In a way, it makes sense. In a way, it might be the most honest thing that's been said on the matter. A shunning of history one can't help but love. Maybe it's not about purity in that sense—maybe it's because a person can't live with that much time, that much past to *skirt around*.

Discovering the video a few weeks later he snatches the camera out of her hand and fends her off with an outstretched elbow. Give me that. He studies the film, his eyes soften like a wound. He becomes hospitable. His body, oblivious to being observed. He asks about that scene—it's evening and they're seated in the kitchen having spaghetti. What scene.

The one she told him about, the one with the breast.

What about it.

Is that what it was like, he wants to know. He's talking about Duras, that film with the very lengthy shot of a naked woman in it, the breast of a woman asleep. You think you're looking up into the crown of a tree, only to discover that what you're seeing aren't branches at all, but the photographed capillaries of a heart. A wrist, a body transilluminated. The way things fall together, a pulse turned into something you can see.

Who was she out with.

No one.

Limping, hobbling home, the fir trees parting like scarlet lips; a leg dragging behind, the way a cat might drag itself home, hind leg trailing like a broken cart. The horse was down by the meadow, tossing its head, the reins tangled up in the branches, only then it wrenched itself loose and set off at a trot, bridle dangling from the headstall, following the perimeter of the colts' enclosure. The green of confusion, the vegetation, the last hours of afternoon. A group of girls stopped what they were doing and dropped their currycombs, or else simply stood and stared; a couple of them came running towards her, clambering over the fence, and as they reached the wood and the girl, she fell down in front of them, like a heavy sinker when the line is released, plummeting to the bottom, an anchor descending through current, all the softer strata, motion in the direction of the horizon. The wind picked up and passed over them like waves rolling in from the open fields, a rotten stench of sea borne upon the air, slabs of mingling perception, rising up in a murmur, lapping this far or that, issuing its sighs and sinking to the ground, to whisper in the gravel, in the sand, and the wounds. Her freckled skin was gashed apart, arms blotched with blood, blood trickling from her nose, and an eyebrow glistened red. In the far field they attended her, tearing open her long-sleeved T-shirt, its weary fabric relenting at once. Her arm was at an angle, the bone stuck out from the middle of her forearm, the lower part with the hand dangling like a decoration. There was a lot less blood than one would have thought. Her leg, her leg, the girls cried out in unison, then busy whispers exchanged, endeavours to make her comfortable, to arrange her in some way that resembled a natural position of the body. And all the time thwarted by some issue, knees that refused to bend, and the sight of her eyes as they flickered in shock.

Her face was the worst, but no one saw.

And the internal organs: a lung slowly filled with blood, patches of deepening shadow, fluid seeping darkly from the body.

Help is on its way, they assured her.

Someone had phoned.

The horse had stepped on her face, the left side, a loose tack in the shoe had gashed her open from just above the eye, a fleshy flap hung from the socket, her apple cheek parted like the tall grass of the meadow through which they rode.

Who was she out with.

The horse lowered its head, came to a halt, snorted into the soil, turned, lowered its head again, and nibbled absently at the couch grass. The flap, flap of horse lips smacking together, the moist rending of pasture detached by the teeth.

She gazed up at the tops of the fir trees, they pointed up like mountain peaks that strove towards the sky, and all movement was suddenly directed upwards, she felt; the fall had lasted an age, but when first she let go and allowed herself to tumble she thought fleetingly of the speed at which everything hurtled towards the clouds, the whistling rush of the air; she hit the ground at the edge of the bridle path hollowed out over time by the tramp of hooves, twisting round in mid-flight as she was hurled under the horse's hind legs. Now she tried to move her arm, but couldn't, and found the other to be likewise unresponsive. Blades slashed at her like darting swallows beneath the ridge of a roof; she wanted to know about her face, but not a sound would leave her mouth. She's trying to say something, one of the girls realised, commanding her friends to shush; they could see only the right side of her face, the left was seen by no one.

The body, opening itself.

They stood and listened, watching her lips. *Face*, the girl whispered, *face*, repeating the word several times, and everyone understood, yet no one spoke.

They saw the ambulance—and three weeks later her face. It looked like a field, skin sewn together in a patchwork of boundaries and trampled-down tracks. Part of the jaw was saved, three teeth, the cheek rebuilt from bone grafted from the radius. For a long time following she was blue, and they shot the horse, it was too wild to ride, too *afflicted* to be kept in any place. Castrated too late, it was like it never realised it wasn't a stallion anymore, they said. The girls understood that to a point, but everyone agreed that shooting it was best, on account of that face. Its eyes darted in their sockets as it was led out into the farmyard so they wouldn't have to move it as far once it was dead. The gunshot was a whirle in the air—dust, grass seed, sand.

All language is a translation of something.

The leaves of the chestnut tree, the way they unfold from the bud in the space of a few days in early May, are a translation.

A man stands in the middle of the road and two dark-coloured cars sweep past him very closely, one on each side, moving in their opposite directions. He has to turn sideways so as not to be hit. His body mirrors in the paintwork and the windows, the rush of wind as they pass causes the hairs on his arms to tremble. The particular hang of a dress. The minutest of movements in the region of an eye—industry. A translation.

Roots in poor soil, sandy soil, meagre.

You appear on the path beneath the chestnuts and have lost weight from all your worries. It suits you. The compactness of your body, the fact of being able to see what's under the skin. Your hands are in the high pockets of your short-cut coat, so your arms stick out like wings, two triangles in your wake. You greet me, and later you say something about selling at a loss. I can't remember what it was you meant, only that it seemed plausible that it should be so.

I put my hand out and thought how fleshy it looked.

Everything is a translation.

You shook my hand and it felt like a reconciliation. You held a cigarette between your fingers while it disintegrated into ash. We walked in the direction of your nod. I imagined how he would look sitting in my kitchen.

I'm going to Fyn, you say. Your eyes have different colours from the trauma. You want to go the limit, you say. You say you're not sure if I understand you when you say you're tired, I'm tired. You'd rather crash out in style than not give it a go. I think you're right about me not understanding. I want comfort—but right now it seems like it's not going to happen.

You look at your watch and the sky. It's our own fault, you point out. We sit down on the slope and watch the swans. They put their cheeks to the wind in turn, first one then the other, like sails. We're both speechless—the choreography of it is like a symbol. The lake changes colour from blue-violet to deep blue, shifting in a matter of seconds—three, four, a mere blink of the eye. Eight swans, now in a circle on the lake. The lake is not an eye. We tramp out a path on our wanderings around it, deeper and deeper.

What is the relationship of the body to the voice. Prayer, declaration, oath, song, elegy, ode, allegory, novel. How can a voice be retained, how much can be altered without the voice becoming another. Nothing is ever the same. Therefore, there is no comfort nor any argument in favour of us being together at this moment; no reason *we* should be together.

Tone is determined by distance.

Keep talking to me.

The dying fruits hang and wither, folding themselves up into a wind harp of origami skulls. Fungus spores spread on the wind, are scattered by wind, rain, insects; flies carry the microscopic spores from fruit to fruit. The bruised fruits are the ones assailed. The biting, sucking insects, the grubs that bore, the wasps that gnaw, the birds that peck, and the hail that beats and batters—all opening up their points of entry. And the untended apple trees whose apples have been left to flourish cheek by cheek, so bountiful the fruits hang almost in bunches—these are the trees to be attacked. The spores wander from last year's hollow fruits to the new of summer. And we see it happen. We see our woman sit down in the grass, and we see the man remain standing with that rake.

The straw hat—where did the straw hat come from—casts a shadow across my eye. A sandbank where amber and flatfish absorb the sun in shallows of warmth.

We see her look down at her hands. She sees herself with his eyes. In his eyes she is not herself.

A pear, a stricken bird dropping to the ground.

By mistake a woman washes a woolen jumper in the washing machine, causing it to shrink—and commits suicide that same afternoon. A man takes his own life after seeing an unfamiliar cat get run over a few hundred metres down the street. Another breaks down crying during dinner, his partner having mentioned Dublin and the holiday they spent there, when they couldn't get a taxi and had to walk four kilometres in the rain. A girl lies sleepless in her room, in tears over having lost a ballpen that was special to her. A woman swallows fifty paracetamols after being handed a speeding ticket.

I have a preference for plainness. Plain make-up. Plain plants—the weeping fig, for instance. The idea of *regular*. When things don't draw attention to themselves and try to be better than they are, or more out of the ordinary, like that. There's enough pageant in the world as it is. Enough showing off.

PROLOGUE

The first thing we see is grey, near-black earth. A warm glow in the blackness, a moistness of colour.

The wind is the only thing to reveal time. Or the gentle arc of the plant in its lean towards the ground is the only thing to reveal time.
The green with the black.
The green against the black.
The image is the softest shudder.
The movement becomes a state. Again, we lose the sense of time into which we had settled.

SCENE I

A bed inside a bedroom. Night. Darkness. On a desk at the back of the room stands a lamp with a lampshade of green glass. The lampshade refracts the light, making it fall like heavy rain. The table is sodden with light, like a forest floor. The light fans out around the lampshade and makes a halo.

Another lamp stands on a heavy foot at the bedside, arching its neck. Its light is harsher. It falls coldly upon the two people in the bed. It is a dusty light that does not enshroud the body but seems instead to peel away a layer of the skin.

Occasional hairs tremble, detached from one another, and every strand seemingly wreathed with light, individually and collectively, halo-like about her face. Illuminated.

The man's face in profile.

We see her features like a sky behind him. Her weightless hair exudes from her scalp and is as kindled by the harsh light.

The white surfaces we know must be the teeth.

Removed and icy, he seems, the way nature can be: indifferent and dramatic at the same time. Pupils darting beneath the thinnest eyelids, partially translucent, the soft wafer-thin hull like the membrane of an egg, quite as thin and yet not as strong—fragile.

THE MAN:

You knew all along.

THE WOMAN:

That there was so little time.

THE MAN:

It's easy for you. You hardly noticed a thing.

Hesitation, revealing a kind of solicitude for him. Or for herself.

The crowns of the trees absorb nourishment from the sky. They too are roots; and roots become crowns in the earth-sky, the worms are insects there.

THE WOMAN:

Do you think that's how it is. That the journey itself exhausts a person. I think it's everything but the journey. In fact, it's more the parting. That, and revisiting what you left behind. The journey is nothing, really.

Your paranoid look.

The woman's throat.

The sweep of the collarbone towards the arm. Goose bumps.

Throat, rising and falling.

And the skin, contracting around the body, the hairs as they rise.

The skin breathes, the body in exchange with its surroundings.

SCENE 2

A tall barstool with shiny, black-varnished legs. A high table in front of the window facing the garden. She sits on the stool, erect: the light is summer's, it is summer, the breeze from the garden tugs at the white curtains that brush the floor like a hand passing over a knee, a disruption inside the room. Summer. The light falls in flat bands through the leaky walls, ribbons of light like swords plunged from all sides into a blade-box: that image, fleeting. And then again: the light, falling in through slats, slicing up the room.

There are no colours. Sun draws the colour from all things. A dimness is all there is, and this insistent light that seems to want in to everywhere. Like jealousy, the way it works things open. It seeps between the woman's teeth, the narrow gap between her teeth. Light floods into the room like piercing jets of water, the shutters holding together the body of light, allowing only so much to pass.

A kitchen, afternoon. Summer.

The tall stool with the delicate, curving legs.

Her hair hiding her face.

The crown of the weeping willow, the one by the lake, hangs like a woman's hair at the water's edge. These lightest of touches, the sun. All the tiny hairs.

A thought that may occur: that this must be the place.

Closer and closer.

A close-up of the woman's eye. It is half-closed, the eyelid covering exactly half the front of the orb.

Her eye, the collarbone, the chest with its ridges. An image of a flower losing a petal. And another. Withered. The two images superimposed.

Nature declared incapable, cheated, for the most part, she too. This is the way we sense her strength. A tough membrane.

Her fingers are greasy, their tips are moist and we glimpse an eye. It glistens in the light.

Her eye, and then her hands.

Only the hands. Cuticles large and white. Fingers wet, vaguely orange.

We search for an explanation in the image. An explanation in simple terms, a sphere colliding with the next.

We find nothing.

Our thoughts make our eyes homeless, our eyes beginning to wander. First within the image itself, then back within our thoughts, and into the image again, for we are unable to escape from the image into abstraction, not here.

We search outside the image and yet within what is seen. We try expanding the space by means of thought—a still larger image. Thinking by visualising.

We find her, for we have marked the place we left her, though not exactly, not the stool, but her body.

A small blue mark, occupation of a country, a flag or a stamp—this is how we occupy her, by leaving our mark on her body. The woman looks up.

We can find our way back to the marked body.

Her hands are placed before her on the table like fish.

She looks out at the garden.

We see the garden as she sees the garden, through the double French doors. They have stayed open all afternoon.

Shimmering warmth, something sugary that makes the dark green seem sticky. We turn our gaze towards her again, study her eyes to see if we saw the same as she.

Her expression is concentrated. She stares into the distance, a very particular concentration that makes us think that she does not see the garden at all. Her expression is that of a person looking out to sea.

A rhythm tapped out by a finger on the edge of a bathtub, the edge of a table, a hard and shrivelled fruit. Waves cross-hatch the sea, the way people cross-hatch landscapes and bodies.

The sea seems to go on for ever. The work of cross-hatching goes on forever.

The rhythm of the work, reminding us of states, other occasions, the memory of something repeated many times, the way you remember a season or a way of existence.

One of her eyes.

And the image of the sea.

We see the two images superimposed.

The two images are equal, there is no hierarchy. Time and place are unimportant, nothing is more imagined than anything else, her eye and the sea are equal because of their salience for us, here.

The image of her eye gradually becomes clearer, more distinct. It seems almost to soften the sea. And behind it: the image of the garden.

We see the three images as one, each superseding the next by turn.

The garden, vanishing.

The garden, vanished.

Her eye now fills the screen and is the only image we see: her eye. A black pupil, mottled green iris, the white of the orb, the only part of the body that is truly white—apart perhaps, in certain cases, from the teeth. Almost invisible, these tiny capillaries; and at the same time we see the ocean reflected in the eye.

We understand: she is looking out across the sea.

We understand: the garden is the sea. The door is not merely a door leading out into the garden, but a door leading out to the sea, both existing at once. The sea, waves.

And then once more: they are bright, a heap of rose hip on the table in front of her.

Not a single stain on her white blouse with its ribbons and lace. Preparing rose hip in such attire. An old-fashioned blouse, it may be very old, an item kept and cared for.

Then the three colours. The green of the garden, the blue of the sea, the orange of the rose hip. The three colours can borrow from each other, her skin borrows colour from it all. And at the same time we realise: in such light, in such heat, colours cannot exist. Everything is either black or white, the season of calligraphy. Not winter, as one might think.

We hear the breeze. We see her ear—now we see only her ear. The image changes, we see the rose hip dissected. The white seeds like teeth.

Her collarbone. And we see the bark of the birch tree up close. The two images melt together and she rises, her chest ridged like the bed of the sandbank, the same metal gleam.

Green eyes.

She has risen and moves towards the door. We see her from behind. We see the garden outside, and at the same time her eye, the sea reflected in its sheen, not distinctly, we sense it to be a kind of disharmony, the kind that is always present in the world.

We see the garden, but then the sea.

The sound is of the sea.

The shift has occurred imperceptibly, the sound of the garden has become the sound of the sea, imperceptibly, and yet within minutes the sound alters again and becomes once more the sound of the garden. Trees. The wind in the birch trees and the aspen.

The sound of light and wind passing through foliage. Through tall grass that has not been cut for a whole summer and a whole spring. This is the movement that carries the shift in sound, from the garden to the sea, the trees, that are the sound of both, always. And then: the heap of rose hip.

The halved rose hips, rinsed and cleansed, in a bowl of black enamel that is matte on the outside, shiny inside.

The colour of rose hip dulls the senses.

SCENE 3

A wide beach, the sky. And the sea, slicing the image in two, as a revelation might, or an involuntary insight into the way something hangs together.

To lose something one never thought could be lost.

There are no sounds from the sea, but a person breathing. A sound from a body breathing—lungs, skin, breathing in and out. The beach has emptied, no one remains there, but we hear a person breathing.

At first the breathing of one.

Then two.

Two bodies, breathing.

First the breathing, then voices.

What are you doing here.

The sound of the sea surges in, as if until now it has been contained within a cloth, and then the deluge as the taut fabric is slashed with a knife.

We hear the voice distinctly.

The way it comes in over the sound of the sea, the sound of sand swept by the wind.

The man and the woman move into the frame, they enter the frame, appearing on the screen from the right. They walk on the beach. The steps they take are many.

We watch them walk. We watch them from afar. And then: the heel as it strikes the sand, the release of the toe, the knee reaching its apex, bent, stretched. Again, we see them from afar.

Their voices remain distinct, as if we are very close to them. They make no special effort in speaking, the rush of the sea is a voice apart. In this way the voices stand out, rather like an unfamiliar black wallet left on a dining table. Something on top of something else and shining almost. Now and then a seagull cries, or else we hear the wind at our backs. The wind, buffetting the vegetation, the noise of leaves rustling above their words, allowing us to hear only fragments:

THE WOMAN:
...to get away. It's like there's no room for thoughts when my head is blown full of sand, and that sound, the waves.

She gestures, throwing up her hands, pointing or whatever.

THE MAN:
...the body casts, of the mother and child.

THE WOMAN:
...like that...Pompeii...you know...

We move closer to the beach, venture some metres out into the open space, some metres out into the sand.

THE WOMAN:
The heat there—it's like your throat filling with sand.

She grips her throat with both her hands, forming a collar that rises towards the jaw.

THE MAN:

They were so small.

THE WOMAN:

Something they weren't meant to see, something stolen, something you steal your way into seeing, but which maybe you …

THE MAN:

…which maybe you shouldn't have. They look like children dressed up as adults. And the children look like animals dressed up as human beings.

THE WOMAN:

What do you remember.

THE MAN:

I remember the body casts, of course, the one of the mother and child. That's mostly it. But then I come to think of all the living, draining their water bottles as they wait for the train back along the coast. Water bottles strewn all over the place. And their faces, the gravity written all over them, the understanding that it would be wrong to laugh, that gravity is the appropriate thing, to be weighed down like that. And they think: I'm glad to have seen this, and glad to be able to go home again and forget such images. The beach, the rocks, and the sea—I suppose that's what they thought about. Tomatoes and lemon trees, lemon liqueur, lemon soap.

We see the sea. The two people have left the frame again, the man and the woman. They continue to speak, we hear their voices.

THE MAN:

A thin dog.
A lost child.
A despairing face.

THE WOMAN:

Did you see their mouths, the way they were open. You can almost hear them, can't you.

They've been screaming for seventeen hundred years, interred in the form of cavities. Before eventually they were discovered and had plaster of Paris poured into their forms. I think of it like developing huge photographs, only in three dimensions. The plaster is the developer poured over the photographic paper in a darkroom. I don't think you can deal with looking at them unless with that thought in mind—that they're empty shells to us, reconstructions, like shadows of something you … you have to misrepresent, and see for what they are.

THE MAN:

They were all running, that's what I remember best. I imagined the way they tried to run away from the cloud of ash. Children in their arms, legs bent, that kind of thing.

THE WOMAN:

I can't think at all when I'm there, I'll never learn how. It's like everything dissolves as soon as I set eyes on the place, like it won't present itself as something real, it's a problem. All thoughts kind of disappear—whoosh—just like that, reduced to nothing.

We hear the clack of two pebbles and understand that she has paused to pick them up and throw them into the sea, or else keep them in her pocket, or walk with them in her hands.

SCENE 4

The boy sitting on that person's knee, that must be him.

In the photo both his front teeth are missing. In another he is standing in cotton underwear, white underwear, on a quiet residential street. He's got big leather boots on and in his hand is a leash that droops away in an arc towards a dog the same size as the boy himself. His eyes haven't changed, but everything else has.

His face has shifted in some way, it's the same face only different. Like the autumn, summer, death, is merely a passage, like all things. In the process of becoming the same only different. Nothing can be held up and compared. Contradictions don't exist.

A beach, raked and made tidy in the night—next morning everything is different. He emerges from the mudroom.

She is the only family he has left.

His uncle and the others, who in a way vanished along with his father back then. They were in the boat.

The yearning for a time one no longer recalls. There is a white orchid in the window, its flowers are three quiet parasols in the sun. Muffled sounds of activity from the kitchenette. A sink with a visible drain that disappears into the wall, a bar of lavender soap, the smell issuing into the room, keeping its walls upright, the ceiling in place.

His rented room.

THE MAN:

Her cheek was gashed, she smiled out of her cheek. Her eye had been attached to its socket, but both eyelids, lower and upper [he points at the woman, puts his fingers to her eyelids, lower and upper at once], were kind of split open vertically and had retracted from the eyeball.

THE WOMAN:

A film about two women, an actress. She stops talking.

THE MAN:

I've seen it. It's brilliant.

THE WOMAN:

Atonement, was that it.

THE MAN:

I think it was *Persona*.

Their bodies, skin against skin. The violet tinge of the shadows, where an arm angles like an Italian stone pine (the slender trunk with its dramatic twists, the way you turn your head away suddenly in horror, an arm resting on his abdomen; various details, dark hair, a nipple with surrounding lactiferous glands, a hand, tendons visible through transparent skin stretching across the back of the hand, a knee, the rear of the knee where veins run close to the surface of the skin.

THE MAN [looking at the plant]:
It's doing fine. Look at the flowers, they're still there.

He strokes her hair to reassure her or himself. She is nervous, thinking about their parting, thinking about the way it feels like a countdown; she is unsure as to whether she will miss him.

If he will mean anything to her.

THE MAN:
It's fine, it needs watering, that's all.

They lie still and we see them from the side. Their legs look long. They are looking in the same direction, his hand comes to rest on her head like a shadow that won't go away.

Some time passes. The sun moves across the sky, shafts of light escape through the layer of cloud and slant into the room. On the street outside, people pass by, a young woman with her grandmother, the obvious annoyance of having to take care of the aged.

THE WOMAN:
Are you asleep.

THE MAN:
Yes.

THE WOMAN:
I miss you already.

THE MAN:

You're tired, that's all. I'm right here.

THE WOMAN:

She fell through the window.

The line of her back against the sheet. A split image, like an eye bisected by an eyelid. The shimmering violet where sheet meets skin. The work of gutting a fish, the palm of a hand pressing it flat against the board.

The image dissolves with a shudder into a tableau of metal, tin. Some discarded roofing panels, variously grey and rust-red, tinged with green. Another dissolve, and we see her skin, the sheet, the sweeping line of her cheek, like a travelling droplet of moisture. Dissolve: tin, roofing panels. Dissolve: skin and sheet.

Eventually, the two images replace each other so quickly that all we see is an abstract shimmer. The breathing of the two people grows louder and increasingly abstract, dinsintegrating. The faintest of sounds amplified, the image changing too fast for us to discern any single element.

Thus we leave the scene:

The two figures mid-stage in the bed, the spinning storm of images, the sound of their breathing as it turns into the sound of the sea; or the sea being the sound of their breathing, a sound such as that produced by pressing one's fingers hard into one's ears, or closing one's eyes and listening.

SCENE 5

We see a gleaming, white-painted floor of wood. Long curtains drape wave-like, sweeping in the breeze in front of the open door. On the other side of the door: blue where there should be green. The garden is blue. But there are sounds of a garden in summer, a bird. The low hum of agricultural machinery in the distance.

THE WOMAN:
Are you asleep.

No one answers, the room is quiet. A cat comes in through the door and passes through the room like a pair of scissors through a length of fabric.

THE WOMAN [again]:
Aren't you going to wake up soon.

No answer.
Time.
Now and again the curtains are lifted from the floor entirely, the breeze is gentle, the lightness of the curtains is like a woman who has not eaten in months, half-years, that same bluish tinge, the down that covers her skin, a lightness of movement and a peculiar masculinity as the bones, the jaw, the skeleton become visible.
The lightness that resides in that.

THE WOMAN:

I remember I was going to pretend to be asleep. I've forgotten the reason, if there even was one. I suppose there
wasn't, apart from the desire not to…miss out on that
special kind of solicitude, or whatever you might call it;
the tiptoeing about when people saw I was sleeping. I
wanted to hear that. The way people's movements become
cautious, as if they were actually walking on top of me like
on glass or nails. The look in their eyes, without sound.
But I woke up, it was evening by then, and all the guests
had gone home.

I don't know…I could tell they'd been there and had cel-
ebrated my birthday without me. It was for me they'd
come—and perhaps they carried me into the other room.
Had I really been asleep, rather than just pretending.
Are you asleep.

THE MAN:

Hmm.

THE WOMAN:

Please don't.

A sound of crisp sheets, as if the bed were made of the dryest straw
or paper, when the body settles.

We see the fabric, the skin, as the duvet is drawn aside. Their
bodies are a single beast, sleeping.

THE MAN:

What were you thinking when you bought this place.

THE WOMAN:

Were you there that evening. Did you see me.

THE MAN:

It was because of the garden, wasn't it.

THE WOMAN:

And did you leave then. Couldn't you see the difference.

THE MAN:

The difference between what.

THE WOMAN:

Real sleep and…

A woman's hand cuts into the lower frame. The hand is slender, the fingers long. Tendons flex beneath the skin. It rests lazily on the shiny white of the painted wooden floor.

THE MAN:

Hmm.

THE WOMAN:

…pretend sleep. That…goes wrong.

A silence. The woman crawls naked on all fours across the floor, reaches out and grasps the bottom rail of the French door to pull it shut.

A hand reaches out to clutch her leg. He grips her ankle and she pulls free.

> THE MAN:
> We've only just met. You keep forgetting.
> Sleep now.
> Can't you sleep.

> THE WOMAN:
> I don't think I can.

The woman is making up a story about him, a story about the remnants of an encounter.

You're tired, we walked I don't know how many kilometres along the shore, you must be tired.

We see the woman hold a hand up in the air, opened like a fan. She turns her hand as if considering a prism. The ceiling lamp's severe splay of light against the wall.

An image of the wall: the figure of the fan. The graphics contained in the movement of the hand, fingers like slats.

The alienation that can arise all of a sudden, as abruptly as the opposite arose.

Everything can be reclaimed, it's so obvious here.

The mobility of bodies, thoughts. One minute—the next.

That collapse and the resurrection into something like: togetherness. One, a union, without end, and yet always ending.

SCENE 6

A glowing coal he suddenly holds in his hand.

The sun squeezed into a black ball. Wishing for something, or wanting something.

SCENE 7

In rain. A summer, everything threatening to burst into flames at any moment. Bonfires and watering are banned. All glass is forbidden, mirrors are, tin foil, gold leaf. Garden waste piling up, because we want things tidy too, and the hedge needs doing. We want brand new views, we want *vistas*. If we dig up all the bushes on the hill we'll be able to see the sea from the decking. And he might, you might have gone back to your parents.

If only they could cut down those trees, the cluster of trees that block a view you remember from when you were a child.

The view comes creeping forth.

And we dream again of rain.

The late sun has to ignite a whole landscape, though it's nearly on fire already, and of its own accord.

Burning.

And then it comes. A drop that strikes a cheek or a warm arm. And then the next, and the next again, and all at once the sky rips open, rain pours down on us, plastering heads of hair to scalps, nature opening wide its mouth, gaping gullets, all drains and ditches, clothes, skin and veins are vessels greedy for rain.

In the towns, water fills the streets.

It travels across the road in its patterns of herringbone, washing with it a jetsam of newspapers, plastic, matchsticks, and still it falls, heavy drapes of fabric hung from the sky. The streets are overflowing, the rain rising up above the kerbs, to the doors of the houses. It seeps into their entrances, trapping the people inside, who stand and watch while the water floods in like light under their doors.

A single door, opened slowly.

We seek the high ground, clambering onto furniture. That kind of rain. And maybe eventually you manage to enter your building, you let yourself in, press open the door, step into the hallway, close the door behind you. The encroaching water, so quietly it flows. And slowly you realise: this isn't where you live, this is the wrong apartment. Yet you take off your coat and walk through the hallway, into the living room, to kiss a woman who has no idea anything is wrong. Or a woman who doesn't think anyone will come, that all are drowned, and that either she takes this man or no one at all. This may be reasonable. Arbitrariness is a fact we must live with, a fact we live with regardless of any other circumstance. Presumably that would be the kind of thing such a woman might think.

Dryshod first.

Nice, shiny black, patent leather shoes. Round toes. And she goes into the kitchen to see to the dinner. Maybe she leans across the counter and sees her distorted face reflected in some surface. Maybe she speaks her name out loud, in fact she does, she whispers it so that you may not hear. She listens with eyes closed. The way he takes off all his clothes and puts on those of a stranger instead. Your transformation can be seen in the woman's face too. Her face changes. It's what faces do, change with every new person they love.

My face is your face.

We decide to make love. My face is your face. And when she opens her eyes, her eyes have become white.

She closes them again.

When she opens her eyes, they are black.

The entire orb, black.

She tries again, and now they are blue, they are acceptable.

Borrowed new eyes, and yet seemingly so—and this is the word she thinks—REALISTIC. We realise this is important to her, to live a realistic life, whatever that is. And when she puts a dish of steamed fish down on the table, she thinks to herself: This is a realistic fish. These are lovely potatoes, he says later, and she thinks: This is a realistic thing to say. At this point in time it's realistic that he say such a thing. Compliment her on the food. And their entire life together can be realistic, she thinks. The thought comforts her. The fact that she can ENVISAGE it being so.

And so she is reconciled.

Everything that may be seen, and everything that may be envisaged, and everything that nearly exists. It all runs together in her mind. Whatever difference there might be. Whether it matters. You drink wine. You talk. She confides in you, and you nod as if you understand. Or maybe you really do understand her. Maybe she really is the one you have always loved, maybe she's the one you were always looking for in your girlfriend. Who would go looking for someone they never knew. I suppose that's what occurs to me—that you never knew the one you loved. Only nearly.

The woman switches on the light and we see the man has lain down to sleep with his head in her lap.

She strokes him, we see his hair, her fingers at first trembling, then becoming steady.

The scene draws out, slowly, slowly.

The woman's hand moves with increasing weariness, heavily it proceeds across his skin, comes to a standstill, then jolts abruptly into motion again. All this is seen in close-up. There is nothing else in the frame than this hand and the trail of light that traces its movement. It's like seeing the hand and the night through the sights of a rifle. As if one could blow the two people away with two shots and put an end to it all. We feel empowered, a feeling superseded by something like: the sense of having no power at all over anything. Impotence. That kind of feeling. Being subordinate to the two bodies. While eyes might be imagined that can see in the dark, one can never imagine a human body that does not at some point fall asleep. To be trapped in the body. Though perhaps in the proximity of another, a real body next to one's own, or perhaps on top. The feeling that this possibility exists. To lie in one bed, two people; to lie there all four, five, six. Riddled with holes and alone, an insane multitude.

THE WOMAN:

You know, I was thinking, that when I met him it was like something happened to time. I never got older. Not by a single day, not until he left me. The year after.

The woman puts her hands to her face and explores her skin.

THE WOMAN:

And then you wake up [she repeats] and your face is the same as two, three, four years before. Then straight away, at a single glance, the body ages. Just like that. Like a skin sloughed off, as if the realisation of standing still precipitates collapse. A kind of hideous unmasking. You've yet to see what damage it did, the time that was spent together. And then there you stand, with the wreckage of your face.

You think: I can't ever see anyone again, not with this face.

THE MAN:

You think the whole world will turn away. But then.

THE WOMAN:

But then no one can tell. Your face has looked like that all the time, and you're the only person not to have noticed.

THE MAN:

That may be the most terrifying part of it. Those around you never letting on.

THE WOMAN:

And so it turns out you don't know a soul in this world. The fact that they saw nothing. Said nothing. Or the fact of you not hearing.

SCENE 8

A bed, in the middle of the room. The man and the woman tightly entwined.

A tangle of arms.

Sleeping.

Only a blue sheet covers them, or rather: it has slipped partially from their bodies and hangs to the floor like water running over the lip of the bathtub in their hotel room. Like honey spun from the comb—a limp disarray of arms and legs, and blue light. Night, or early morning. Summer. We see them on their stage, from the audience, and from above.

A film, the movements made in the course of a night.

Images bleeding into each other, a night of poses edited together, physical arrangements, more or less: a single body. At least: a single movement. And at the same time: the image of a hand.

We understand the person is asleep.

The hand of a woman asleep.

The navel, and the suggestion of her sex; her hips.

The image remains, longer than we thought we wanted it to. The light is soft. We see the throb of her pulse in the neck's artery; and through every image a persistent crackle, the sound of something ablaze, and yet not. It is a human sound, a sound of the body, though uttered in language unintended to refer to anything else. The sound of a body when consciousness is rendered unconscious by the truth of sleep—unchoreographed sleep.

EPILOGUE

An image of the lava pouring down the slopes of the volcano's cone.

Plants withering in the heat. It's as if the volcanic soil is being fed. The heat chars everything, makes everything its own.

An image of a blackened landscape.

The volcano sleeps, the lava stark and solidified. Everything is burnt. We see what must be the remains of the green plant. We remember it. There's a kind of grief over time having passed. The picture is still, without movement. After some time something stirs, dust being shifted by what we can only take to be the wind. The charred plant pulverises in the disruptive air. We see what used to be plant, disintegrating in that way. Dust whirls and settles, a fine mantle of black on the stage. The woman must close her eyes for the dust not to make them dry and lustreless. The man shields her face with his hand. Covers her mouth. He shuts his own eyes tightly.

We watch as the woman rises to her feet, removing the man's hand from her breast; she rises slowly from the bed and steps out of the light, passes through the dimness, to a table behind the bed. The murk is green and soft. We see her body become another in the green.

Light has age.

That's what hurts about light, and what is uplifting about darkness.

The body understands this.

She examines some papers that are spread out on the table. With this act, time passes.

The body adjusts to all things. The body accumulates time. The body takes in the time of light.

The morning light is 8.3 minutes old when it is shed upon our faces. We absorb this time, becoming older and older still, depending on the amount of time that is shed upon us.

If we stay in the dark it's different.

But the fact you had to go home again. Or me having to stay. There are various chairs in the room. We see their silhouettes, along the wall and drawn out onto the floor. The shadows they cast. The house is by the sea, slightly back from the shore. A hundred metres, or a hundred and ten, a hundred and twenty. Depending on the tide and the storms. A small patch of grass out front, juniper. Dark, green sloe. Heather, dry grass. We see the house on a summer's day, a face, a boy reading. His eyebrows are knitted close and look like the leaf of a fern, the same shape, widest towards the middle of his face, a slender, freckled nose. It is the height of summer, the dreadful spring has passed, endured. Now the days run together, the way light can run together with things that radiate, the same light, one day and the next.

The approaching of a point, a place in the woods, simultaneously from two different positions.

The darkness of night is no longer darkness, more an inky kind of light, a bluish rendition of daylight, as it is here on this night, with the sea's fog descending upon us. An odd collapse of time, like a row of books on a shelf, the glue of spines vanished and gone, the threads of bound volumes rotted away.

A form that surrenders and leaves its elements to stand on their own.

The being unable, incapable of maintaining standards, the way you might give up on what is done and what is not and simply hang the washing out on the balcony to dry.

A whole human, when thoughts dislodge and drift away from the body's pain—this is what we hold up to the light and examine, this is what we see. Okay, so this is what happens.

An outpouching of a spinal disc, the fluid that seeps, pressing against the nerve, like when she went to open the back door for the first time after her long trip, a shove of her shoulder against the rail, a gummy complaint from the rubber beading, the wood that had contracted and expanded so many times since she had been there last. Where have I been—where have I been all this time. Time, accumulated in all the spaces, the gaps in between. Between her lips.

The spine, not only holding the limbs in place, but also upholding a relationship between an arm and a point in the brain.

The different parts of the face, merging. The spine, the books on the shelf—when the first page succumbs, and then the next, a wing whose feathers loosen and dislodge one by one, dropping to the floor like birds shot down from the sky, or stumbling horses. Time as a frail form, the scenes that dislodge from time, whirling in descent. Some words that tear themselves loose and keep returning.

The man and the woman are present in the apartment. They have breakfast. He is going back to the place they met, he says it's a year ago now.

She turns the empty eggshell in the egg cup, as she does every morning.

That we should meet there.

One always expects some sort of payment in return from the world, signs perhaps—coherence, or some kind of solicitude.

Outside, and behind her, a pigeon pecks at a scrap of tin foil on the decking. We see it from the man's viewpoint. The tin foil flashes light into the room, a window of light that disturbs his vision. His eyes moisten and run. He blinks, though without turning away.

The sound of the pigeon is foregrounded, while the camera focuses on the woman—her fingers as they turn the egg, the way she positions the egg cup at the centre of her empty plate, as one might place a tower on a town square.

She finds churches tiresome. The exceptions are bombed churches, those derelict or being restored.

The sound of the egg cup against the plate, the sounds of a kitchen. There's something human about the apartment. The way it breathes in the background. It doesn't feel like a whole year, he says.

She wonders if this is what it's like to be old, not really understanding that so much time has passed. She picks at the egg, the shell white as the white of an eye, faintly speckled, or tarnished—that's the word that occurs to her: tarnished.

Her parents always bring a dozen eggs with them when they come over from Jutland. And a jar of preserves and an orchid. They are fine gifts, she thinks. Simple, yet fine. The thought she had before about old age is too obvious, she thinks now, banal. She would never utter it out loud. But then he does instead, as if to spare her the embarrassment.

I can see she's unhappy about having to leave. She doesn't want to go back.

But it's not the going back she's unhappy about—it's the opposite.

Leaving, never to return. And you think I'm scared of flying, which is touching in a way. You put off going to work, because I'm flying that far—across the Atlantic.

The engines quieten abruptly, and for a moment she thinks: they had a year together.

What does she feel at the thought.

We see her lips, the way the lower lip is curled back into her mouth, the way she bites tiny flakes of skin from its surface. First one side, then the other. It might be understood as concern, but it could be anything.

The house by the sea is hers. It's a thing she owns. It looks like something that found its way onto the land, washed up like wreckage tossed on the surf, that critical point where the waves are as tall as the water is deep and break at the crest, break and break and break.

She connects waves with a variety of things: Virginia Woolf, death, summer, loneliness, conquest. She thinks it's the most pathetic list she can imagine, but there is nothing to be done about it. Dedications, epitaphs.

There are different kinds of recollection, but she is not interested in making any kind of division. It interests her less and less. The opposite makes more sense, finding a common denominator that brings things together.

If there isn't enough light in a room, the picture will be blurred or non-existent.

The available light is not inexhaustible.

If there isn't enough darkness in a room, outlines will be erased, faces extinguished.

The available darkness is not inexhaustible.

The house comes into sight and vanishes with the shifting of day and night.

She's thinking of learning a foreign language, to connect up some more regions of the world.

The house is built on top of a slope. Its tall wooden panelling is painted white. We see a man's hand, fingers held flat, a sparse dusting of dark hairs over the wrist. Tendons beneath the skin. The fingers travel over the painted panelling, pausing near-imperceptibly at every join in the wood. We study the nail of the index finger. The cuticle is the same colour as the panelling—this is what we recall, or else the body recollects, though as a dream retained inside, the reappearance of something, like a person you've seen somewhere before but can't quite place, a thought encountered in a book, something you felt, only not in any language that was able to absorb and retain, a language open at both ends, through which things merely pass, a language unable to save. One can always see what's in a person's eyes, if only one's own reflection. Shiny surfaces can do that, reflect the self, whereby they are the truest nightmare. The constant reminder, the casting back, all those ideas and fantasies.

Many of the trees have been cut down, the trunks already sawn up, ready to be loaded and driven away.

The estate owner is quiet on the phone. I tell him how much it would mean to us—me and my boyfriend.

He yields and concedes that he has been out looking for the tree too, or at least his daughter has, after I sent him my description of where it stood. The pale pink stones you collected on the beach and placed at its foot. We arrange for me to stop by and show him the spot next time I go to Fyn.

I wonder if you will think of it as the gift I want it to be. Or as me trying to write myself into a story in which I don't belong. Picking at the bark. I wonder what kind of instinct is at work inside me. Whether I'm nostalgic on behalf of others, or a para-site on their suffering, dependent on the yearning for things lost, recalling the past to such an extent I recall even those of whom I have no recollection and whose histories with me I gradually invent, remembering in advance. There's a thing called *false memory syndrome*. I don't know what to make of it. I know a lot about wanting to be a part of something. I know everything about standing on the outside, misting up windows with my breath.

The sea is gathered at the bottom of the picture and one could think of the picture as a container—it could look like that; the sea flooded into it, from some leak in the sky, an expanding basin inking in a horizon, reminding us of something we knew but couldn't pin down and still can't find words for.

The two people, the man and the woman, perched on wooden uprights at the jetty, waves lapping beneath them. We see them against the light. In the sunset they're just a pair of silhouettes, feet dangling like the heads of wilted flowers, cumbersome weights.

The sea has promised nothing, and as such it is uncapricious. It swells without will, witholding nothing, revealing nothing, devoid of any narrative, simple or complex, that could cause confusion.

We see an arm reach out—there is a gap between them and they must tip their bodies towards each other like jugs in order to join.

The sun torches her forearm in two just above the wrist, like some accessory come apart, a rope giving way at its weakest point having chafed against an iron mounting, the snap of webbing in the upholstery of a chair, the resultant disintegration that spreads like a creaking, crackling fire. If you put your ear to it you can hear each and every thread, succumbing. If you retreat from someone you love, eventually you will hear only the tiny popping of blisters as they burst. If you put your head under water, you will hear only air rising in small and insignificant pockets, invisible to the human eye. Whatever it is. The microorganisms, the flies. Everything contains the possibility of seeing things in new ways. Thus the revolution—the potential of all things resides in ourselves. The way we see, or maybe the viewpoint from which we see. What heights may be scaled, what graves dug for the self.

We see them from the quay, perhaps from the vantage point of a tall stool—a barstool, say.

His breathing is unsettled. We hear that.

The stutter of his chest as it rises and falls, and yet at the same time the exactness of it. We see an unbuttoned shirt, a spray of dark hairs on a chest. We see him from the front, he shadows our skin. It takes a moment for the eyes to adjust—at first everything is black, the particular blackness of backlight, that contains all colours. He taps a finger against the ridge of another; unlike his breathing the sound is without rhythm, exploratory, human in its tone, an amalgam of wood and teeth. The sea is charcoal grey, silver, and orange, speckled as a heavy fish whose scales parry the sun and send it ricocheting in all directions, causing structures to shimmer. She does not sigh. We hear only the sound of her breathing now. She lowers her hand and places it in her lap.

A close-up of the hand, the thumb folded in the palm, like a jewel or a bone picked clean. The skin against the blue fabric, the structure of the skin, a topographic map, tiny dashes of purple and grey, the pink tinge of the knuckles, some veins. Lines of the skin, lines of a map, contours marked with elevations.

Waves break against the uprights.

Sea spits at the woman's toes, the man's leather soles. The city is a backdrop, a shawl at the moment before it is drawn around the shoulders. The city's heart-rending solicitude, the disconcerting rumble of the metro, an anxiety of nature, that in all other respects knows no such symptoms of chaos. That patent love of simplicity.

The silhouettes. The two figures on the wooden uprights of the jetty.

I spoke to that girl again, you know the one. I helped her boyfriend once. I don't know why I'm telling you, you're not supposed to know.

She turns her head and lowers her eyes, perhaps as a sign for him to continue, it's hard to tell from a distance, but whatever it is he goes on:

I helped him win her back. All I did was state the obvious in writing. He couldn't find the words himself.

No.

What he meant.

A pair of heavy waves roll in from a passing ferry. They draw their feet up, the way you draw children to your chest at a busy road, the way you hitch up a long dress to cross over puddles.

What do you want me to say.

His eyes turn hard, like horn or bone. He looks up at the sky, throws out his arms in an angular gesture. Bird-like, the way he sometimes is.

The horse lowered its head and trotted flat-backed off into the ruffled landscape, disappearing from sight behind the barn. They could hear the hollow thud of its hooves against the ground, their familiar, graceless rhythm. She looked down at his hands and he followed the arc of her gaze through the air, attentively, the way you might watch a bead travel across a floor before bending down to pick it up. After their fight she feels like her love for him is burning a hole in her pocket.

She doesn't quite know what he *expects* of her.

There's a fatigue, too, that evades capture. I will always think of her as something I failed to let go in time, a burning coal in the hand, a watering eye dripping between fingers, a leak within the world that implants itself in the body, the telephone wires that slice through the poplar, the various patterns of the sky, Lille Strandgade, Skt. Annæ Plads.

He let slip that he used to see a woman who lived somewhere around here.

In that building there.

He pointed up, and naturally she was unable to stop herself from looking, even if she told herself not to, that it was the last thing in the world she needed to do—and the feeling it left them with afterwards as they sat on the edge of the Gefion Fountain was mostly one of no longer having access to each other.

It churned away inside.

What can be gained from overturning a table, dashing a vase. She was beside herself with rage; the scene played out in front of her, and she was her own audience. You've broken our things. He gripped her tight, her wrist. They fought, and for the first time she felt his anger in that way. He wanted to hit her.

Things. For him.

They fell asleep in the afternoon, wrapped up in the duvet, pupated. The cover left marks on their skin. They woke up and made dinner, the day turned on its head. The day unhinged. *His things*. His annoyance at her not treating his things *properly*. Their fight was more about that than anything else. Cutting away the clutter, that's basically what they can't agree on: *things*, the distribution of things, and how to treat them. A battle to behold, own and use.

The horse was out of sight. It stood at the pond, lifted its head, listened.

The horse's eye, with the deformed pupil, not round and smooth like a pebble, but spongy, moss-like, misshapen. He noticed as it stood tethered to the hayrack, the sun angled down and he called for her to come, she was pruning the brambles. She went over, the shears in her hand, heavy like a pistol at her side. Look, he said. And she looked, tilting her head as she did so, pressing her face close to see. Shh, they said, to reassure the horse.

The bike's wheel buckles when in the night we cycle to the sea, unable to sleep. I remember you came home and sat down pale at the table like a theory you suddenly see through but have yet to abandon.

Speaking a foreign language in your own country.

You say you never felt as healthy in all your life, and now you understand your parents.

You're shaken by the attack, though you hardly remember it.

In a way we are all under suspicion. An awning unfolding over a sidewalk.

Deprived areas of the mind, deprived areas of the city.

The rim of the cup is an echo of the moist rim of the eyelid.

She holds the cup cautiously to her eye, lower eyelash resting on the rim of porcelain. Her eyelash, fifty or sixty jointless fingers gripping the cup. The cup, hanging from the flesh like a droplet collected and poised to release.

He calls out and says it's only him.

We see her closed eyes. The daylight is revealing and at the same time anything else but revealing. As if there is a filter on all things, making everything look like something else. Her feet are on the kitchen counter. The room weaves like an old riding-school horse, it scrapes at the sand and tosses its head. The sound of a bridle, the sound of worn leather on worn leather, such heat at two o'clock, such heat at three; the first bell from the church; we see her eyes, startled by the sound, the twitch of the skin around the eye; or the eyelid's collapse at the hammer's strike. The splits and cracks of the epidermis, the contraction of minuscule muscles, like fabric pulled together in little spasms by impatient hands at a drawstring, a thread severed by angry teeth; to disturb such order is a crime; and his body is a gathering storm, a wind yelling down the avenue, collecting up the leaves, collecting up the newspapers with their hideous headlines, collecting up soil and dead insects, sloughed skins, pupae, a gently cupped hand that is the upper section of an empty beehive. Her chest, rising and falling, a wave on the sea running in from two sides, two waves joining together some twenty or thirty metres from shore, like two cold hands pulling off gloves, reaching out and grabbing hold, the white foam at the crest of one and then the other, a mane of colliding momentum, and for a few short seconds the surging rush of union, the way they seemed almost to travel inside each other, like they too once travelled inside each other, a fire seizing hold and galloping across the fields; their two directions becoming one, striving for the shore, that kind of wave; and a chest, rising and falling, trembling, dismaying, its rhythm being the rhythm of the waves; up through the avenue, across the flat expanse, across the beach where the pebbles roll and shift, her eyes, we see them beneath the skin; her eyes, rolling back, a horse taking the bit, tossing back its head, running.

There is such a thing as directionless movement towards each other, and there is such a thing as the opposite: directionless movement away. Outwards, and so on. Grief is without direction, grief seeking out the hollows in this world; so in what forests, in what rooms; nothing to regret, nothing can be endured. Colonies, wastelands of history, a remembered image of avenues of trees in concentration camps without buildings, only trees remaining. The meticulousness of memory as to the items of pain—objects that collect pain and preserve it.

A spoon, for instance, that can't be forgotten.

The thought occurs that memory cannot withstand *things*, that somewhere there's a saturation point, a collapse relating to concrete entities—they become unbearable. The childhood home's presentation of things forgotten, that the conscious mind lacks the strength to carry around on its own, objects bearing witness to our demise, slow and disconcerting, the body becoming brittle and unsound, cells dividing insanely, the blood cleansed no more, hair lost by the tuft or little by little, the nausea, the convulsions of the stomach, the bitter swill of bile that gnaws at the tooth's enamel and eats into the oral cavity, the eyes that cry when they no longer can see the body in which they were set. Homeless eyes, for the body is another; the eyes are the only things whose form remains unchanged when the body becomes—deformed. They can yellow, and be bloodshot.

Two waves we see, that meet and mingle, and surge against the land, a heavy stage curtain drawn up onto the beach, a cool, abundant quilt to cover those who doze, the shells and the creatures, the sand fleas as they spin, thrust here and there on the lather of the sea; blanks blighting our thoughts as we bask in the sun, and soon we are unable to think at all, the mind's every formation shrivelled and forsaken in the bowls of the grief-stricken; implosions of universes, of days that might have been, but never were.

And as she stood there looking out on the sea, it was as if a change in the weather coincided with a voice, and the light transformed, outside and in, becoming colder in the same way.

Admiring the view, he said.

It was like an icy hand gripped her foot as she lay dreaming and snatched her onto the floor. She turned, and there he was. She knew he would be standing there like that, his hand still on the door handle, as if to make his intrusion seem fleeting or coincidental; as if it were *natural*. Yet it was anything but, she thought to herself, and that atrocious comment, too. She decided never to forgive him, the way feelings have to be decided to make them last. It's like what there is on the beach—time engulfs it all, washes it all away; a lump of wood fades and deteriorates, and one day it no longer exists. It's the same with feelings. Whereas decisions endure; they are how countries are governed, and how we govern our lives. The decision takes an emotion hostage and endures, perhaps fading and deteriorating to a certain extent, but still *remaining*.

Can I come in, he says without waiting for an answer.

A bit like colliding with a brick wall in the dead of night when you can't see a thing but think you know the road exactly and can find your way home no problem.

Not even the greatest revolutions change the future as much as they change the past.

A garden of ghost trees, skeleton leaves with the tissue carefully extracted by means of two fingers; the frame of the leaf is soft and moves like hair in water, undulating gently, yielding to the gaze; the figures as they run through the garden, and the wind is a hundred glancing eyes, dusting the scene with a solicitude accumulated from all that the eyes have abandoned, all that has departed them. Tears are the eyes talking about loss. And the eye becomes our only access; the garden itself is an eye, and the stories we tell are all about the eye, what the eye saw and what from it departed. The way the lips move up and down, shaped by our words, and your facial expression when you talk, miming the eyelid's sweep over the orb, again and again. Any kind of movement is a rhythm when considered from a sufficiently distant place. An hour, a day, a life, a millenium. The aspen leaves, tossing like horses' heads in the sun; the sun, reflecting in the eyes, the metal of the bit; the leaves, minuscule mirrors of green throwing back the light, the eyes of the tree. We linger in the garden, longing more than seeing, fidgeting with the past, blinding ourselves, patching thoughts on to everything that is, or was. Turning back again, once more into stone. The milky glaze of the cataract, untreated disease, the years of horses, the march of days, falling into patterns, the way the waves again make patterns, herringbone, or perhaps merely repeating a shoreline over and over again, the outline of a human, over and over again, a hope that he might come and look for me, a hiding place constructed so that you might be found, like in the garden before, when everything was transparent, made so by you, and you were surprised that what I was looking through was you. And therefore I could walk simply past and carry on through the garden, because that's the way many of us are inside.

The fact of never being able to deliver what's asked of you, but always something else instead. The surprise, the *unpredictability*.

A feeble attempt to move on according to one's own designs, and yet: going through motions mapped out for us from the start.

Who is it, you ask. Who is it you miss.

I have come to you beneath the oak tree. The day is darker and cooler here. Tears run down your cheeks. And thus we remain in what was, allowing ourselves no release to enter tomorrow, or even today, in any guise of life. I gaze up into the crown, leaning my head back, opening my eyes.

My father phones and tells me he's wearing a headset. He's in bouyant mood, driving across Fyn. He says he's happy about the weather. I was trying to count all my various texts and had the feeling most would have to be deleted again. I've been thinking I need a system, only then I think I need the system that's already there. My father tells me the students all passed. It's spring, he says. There's no bringing him down. It can be like that a lot—things falling out of synch, an awkward collision of waves, or a boat battered by a rough sea.

I miss the ways of the fields, or the rules that exist. The attention paid every morning on the way to school, my father talking about the fields, the work of harrowing and sowing, the harvest, and what would happen next. The frost, if frost had fallen in the night. The patterns left by the various machinery. The brittle white hoar, the key in which the body is tuned; the *mood* dispensed. I push the blue bead bracelet up my arm and examine the burn. I'm no good at secrets, they seep out of me.

The budgie flies from its perch in the open cage and settles on her head. She has given the bird a name. It belongs to her, a gift. It's a young bird, six months or a year old, blue in colour. It sits on her shoulder when she walks through the village.

She hears her mother pass through the beaded curtain on her way out into the garden.

The bottle with the pear in it, the bird on top of her head, the clack of her mother's wooden shoes; the swish of the beaded curtain as it parts. Straight-backed, she measures across the room to the birdcage and kneels. A gentle nudge and the bird flutters back to its perch. She closes the cage again with a curl of her hand.

She wipes the streaks from her face and follows her mother through the beaded curtain, her mother who is already up the slope and past the apple trees and the woodshed, the heavy washing on her hip in the red plastic laundry basket, her arm angled out to clutch its rim, her torso a tilted counterweight. It's almost midday, and the sun is high in the sky. She starts to run, and the labour of breathing interrupts her sobs. She becomes aware of the fact. The way her body works to find oxygen. Running seems little more than that, using more and more energy in order to breathe, the act of breathing becoming a means of thought, something at once complex and automatic, a state for which one might silently yearn, the motion of the body releasing something inside, something you never knew was stuck.

She catches up with her mother, who holds out her hand. They walk together to the end of the garden, the part that borders the fields.

It will soon be harvest.

They look forward to the smell of harvest, to the mowing of grass and the making of hay; the grass, turned and turned again to be dried, baled, gathered in, stored away for winter. The skin of her legs is like a landscape to anyone close enough to see. Her legs, never fine, forever a patchwork of bruises. Once she counted a hundred. So they say.

You have to adjust to the sound of trees falling.

He takes her hand as though picking something up off the street, something valuable, the claiming of which nonetheless feels embarrassing, but lost is lost, and there it was just lying there. Again she thinks about the way her body always seems to precede her, like a light that can't be caught.

They return to the place where the shards of his father's urn were interred, at the foot of the tree. Each year brings some minor discussion as to which tree exactly. But she knows it's protected now in a way and is glad she could make that happen, at least. The fact that she did something.

How many times a helping hand, how often a shield.

There are no prizes to come back for. That's how it is with spring, there's only so much to go round. The rest is: stumbling. Then winter comes, or just the autumn, as if things weren't bad enough already.

You offer no resistance, and change by the day.

The low dry-stone wall here behind the rectory, the many fruit trees, whose web of roots must be so old and so expansive the cherry trees, the cherries, grow upon the dead.

All is but passage. A new organisation of matter.

In a way, such roots are like the gaze of an eye, looking forward, looking back. Like the two of us, in the midst of these years. It's the oddest age—one feels oneself to be standing on the brink of something, even if that's always true. It's as if something is taking shape, accumulating inside. This dawning conviction. *Almost* having hold of something. Untreated yearning skins over, and sores heal best in the night, when the body is at rest.

Is it a problem, that I'm not sleeping well. Hardly at all, or having these nightmares no one cares to hear about.

We see her standing in the woods, holding his hand. They speak to each other, we see them from a distance. Further and further away. There is a rhythm to everything—considered from afar, that's how it is. The footage from her childhood is characterised by her father's hectic panning shots. His wanting to get as much *in* as possible. The chatter of the two girls can still be heard, the camera panning across the lawn, sweeping by the new chicken coop to the trees at the boundary, the washing line. Almost having hold of something.

Her face twitches almost imperceptibly, as if someone were pulling on a thread fixed to the belly of the sun, a direct line to death or eternity, or some other such thing.

They sleep together in the bed his father died in.

Mushrooms in the field, pasty lips in the fallow, greying grass of winter. A child, a snail's shell lifted to her ear. The leaving of someone, from within to without. The way warmth leaves the body. But you're used to being abandoned, you can sleep anywhere, all you have to do is close your eyes and put something in your ears. Crossing the Atlantic. You're used to it. From within to without.

Sometimes he feels a warmth trickle down his hand. Like a wound opening, the blood coming out. He looks down at his fingers. Turns his hand.

Nothing.

Might pain be a way of exploring the world. Can we look at it like that. We have different ways of feeling things, the way flowers are different depending on whether they belong to someone sick or dead, or to a garden.

His long legs.

Like the gardener, he works nearly all the time.

There's always *something*, he says, people wanting hold, asking him things. And no one ever comes back if he passes their questions on.

Questions, that's what we're left with.

In a way, the past is the only thing we have. Who can say they feel more now than they did then. If you turn and look back for someone, we all know what happens.

The fact that we do so anyway.

Through Aprils we proceed, forever looking back, idling in this fossil state you find me in tonight. Thin is the darkness, spilled between the birches. You say the first eider fowl have laid their eggs at the fjord. You point in the direction, with a wave of binoculars. It's too dark to see, but we can go there tomorrow. I find myself thinking your fingers must get cold. The air has no warmth.

In the night we hear the sound of birds unfamiliar to us. Migrating waders, you say. We hear them more clearly at night. When the wind is spent and the air is a mist. We are calm as far as it goes, and lie here accordingly.

My body precedes me like the beam of a flashlight I carry through these empty buildings, the only light there is.

The snow descends regardless, uncaring of whether we stroll the boulevard or the shore, the snow descends *indifferently*. It can be shifted and cleared, or squeezed into a sphere in the palm of a hand. But from sky the snow merely descends. Snowfall in April, the month of my birth nearly thirty years ago. It's easier to part with something that *is* than something that *was*. Everything we lose remains inside us, while everything we have remains invisible.

The thought occurs to me that the loss I feel can be seen in my eyes, these index cards, place names; all you see are the titles, the rest is in the archive, lining the corridors. In storage. Waiting to be thrown back like the sun as it strikes the pane, across the square, the pond at Agri, a childhood home. The only thing I note at this late stage is that words spoken in love resemble the mutterings of drunks insofar as they are uttered under cover of darkness and therefore vanish with the coming of day, a morning in April, late Easter. Fortunately, some infatuations never pass. Prove me the opposite.

Clasp your hands together. Clasp your hands *like this* into a stirrup.

He prods her with his foot. You can't sleep now.

My mother says everything was fine until we moved out.

We all have our failings.

All the rooms are filled to the brim.

She talks of going on a walking trip, a few weeks. Spain, maybe.

Forward motion. Making the effort to propel the body forward through the snow, though everything feels like you're stuck. The drifts of snow. A black bird on a blue sky. Branches entangled in sky.

Who am I to cause such disturbance.

Twice or more she sees a blackbird pecking at the roof window above the bed, is woken by its shadow on her face, the cooling of her cheek. She is warm when she sleeps.

Others besides her have moved out.

Basically there are two kinds of people. *Me* and *everyone else*.

Inside the *me* is *us*, *we*, *he*, *she*, sometimes a more general *one*.

And then there is *you*. She doesn't know quite what to do with *you*.

An unstoppable return of summer.

He smiles, glancing at the sea and at her by turn. His gaze is a cot in which to rest. Seeing things without being seen. Therein lies the exercise.

I have nightmares, nearly every night.

Incomparable entities do not exist. Everything contains elements of something else. Threads, drawn through the world by the needles of our eyes.

Everything is bleeding.

And everything is still, like soldiers ordered to attention. The language of soldiers is blunt, their words halt like horses at a precipice.

The colours of the birch. This near-violet in the transition from black to white. The colours of marrow.

The children leave animal corpses to steep in a bowl of hydrogen peroxide: mice, a squirrel, a wood pigeon.

They return a week later, coats unbuttoned to the spring. One day I tell you I can't sleep. These days. Bones and skulls, the same pale white as the sky. You nod and strain off the liquid. You suggest coffee.

I nod.

The sound of skeletons in a plastic bag.

Little by little I acquiesce, like winter.

And now it's April.

It's hard to put a finger on what it is that keeps me awake. Thoughts go on in my mind, a variety of interests. My body keeps score in the night, jotting things down on the covers in invisible writing. I get the feeling you could be gone one morning. You've listened to my dreams this long, and to be honest what could be more fatiguing.

Hushful, hushful song of old.

The square, the sight of you lying there on a bench under the linden trees. You were convinced it would all make sense to us *at some point*. The idea of having to go through certain phases to get there. But woods don't always work like that. They come to an end without warning, you stand there teetering on the brink. A feeling of only being joined to the world by virtue of the heel. Sudden clearings; space, air.

The body's exhalation, like a leaf released by autumn. The surrender of the mature.

A thickness of movement.

The letting go of all things at once, like a bundle of pick-up sticks dropped from a hand.

Seedheads opening in the sun.

Something ruptures, and dark-centred serenity spreads inside you.

Pale pink sky. Dark in the centre.

The city, opening.

You suggest something or other.

The sound of seedheads opening in the sun.

The sound of a sapling birch, solitary at the edge of the field, with no history known to us.

The near-violet of the transitions, the days once unfolding, dark and damp in the centre.

The art of the possible—or, as you say, the human circumstance.

To give up the warmth of movement. Something dark and damp, opening with a pop.

The comedy of grief.

Have you given up already.

At very short intervals I feel more *together* than *alone*.

Darkness lets go of morning; a sliding hand, fingers, fingertips ravaged by gravel, releasing the rock; bone-coloured slats of light from a point on the horizon, beyond the sea, projecting into cloud. The light is a body plunging, a flailing in every direction, fingers splayed from a hand, new shoots on the near-dead pear tree at the bottom of the garden, arteries of the heart, glacial streams etching through snow and in the night; the machines at work, light cast electric in snow-spangled beams. High above, on the mountain, the machines trawl back and forth, dragging the inaccessible heights, the snowstorm's impossible, and then: the insane tumult of avalanche. The animals of the peaks toss their heads to the sky amid the yell of all things.

Down in the town: an abrupt awakening in the hotel room, a bare foot pressed into the carpet's pile, a curtain drawn aside, come back to bed. The smallest fluctuation, a shift of the wind, a single degree warmer prompts the snow to release, crystals melting and merging, arms lashed into embrace, we clutch at what we believe to be each other. Curtains of rain travel the sky; vast, overlapping drapes, graphic divisions of light, the repetition of mountains.

The white mountainside, breaking apart, collapsing. Melting ice, dissolving limbs of crystal, or crystal like a cramp-stricken hand folding in on itself in a stagger of spasms. The cloaks of descending snow; a person, two people engulfed by sound, the raucous barrage, arms and legs twisting, snapping like wings wrenched from the carcass, white bone, whiter snow—and then the silence. Hypothermia, and the lungs no longer finding air. One minute, two.

The snow is a firm hand that shields the living.

Sounds veer away and depart. After the avalanche all is still, as still as lime.

Later in the night the machines return to work, smoothing the slopes, clearing the snow among the fir; and up above the treeline, between the red markers, the mountains unfleeced as shorn sheep—another of nature's patterns. The flat ribbons of the pistes, like mesh drawn tight around a tree, an intricacy of scattered tones woven into music: the music of the mountain, to which we listen.

Continuing rumbles of snow.

The bodies are still and buried in snow. A silent, chilly death, crushed beneath a tonnage of weightless crystals, a sky dropped suddenly at the release of a spring, an atmosphere penetrated by stars and planets, descending as dust upon the earth; the life that was changes form, the life to which we are left, again and again. And everything we lost speaks in the stillness of snow.

After the avalanches: this is where we are.

Every footprint is something longed for, hoped for. The town is quiet, a headlamped skier arriving home, a heavy trudge of awkward boots, skis balanced on his shoulder like a stiff wing poking back into the air behind him. He pauses and turns, peers up at the mountain, the lights of the machines that scratch the cornea, etching the contours of the mountain into his eye. His eyes water, and we see his lips, the dryness of days on the mountain, cracked, moistureless surfaces of skin, the creviced flesh of earthquakes and volcanoes, the crust of the earth breaking apart, or the still waters between one wave and the next. As he breathes, a loose flake of skin on his lip flutters in the air, the rustle of a plastic bag snagged in a hedgerow in the wind; his eyes water, rivulets of slime run from his nostrils, descending into his mouth. He turns back towards the road and carries on, the way you carry on the day after a preposterous bankruptcy, the way you sit in the apartment, bent forward, head in hands between your knees, glancing up now and then at the bailiffs as they collect the last of your furniture, and then, finally: the way you have to stand up and let them take the chair from under you; this is how you carry on, boiling water in a saucepan that like you was not worth taking, too insignificant to be of use anywhere else. He sprinkles instant coffee into the saucepan and stares at the patterns it makes, a cream-coloured sky mottled with darker, tarlike clouds. The circular motion of the liquid stirred with a spoon. He turns off the heat and sits down on the floor with the saucepan, leaving it to cool; the distant hum of machinery at work; he picks up the saucepan and puts it to his lips, elbow angled out to the side; he blows into the coffee, watches the rings as they spread, rings of tiny waves, dissipating concentrically into oblivion. His trembling hand, like some pang of jealousy, a cluster of crystals melting together on the mountain, curtains tossed by a wind, bands of snow beneath the clouds, snow on the repeating peaks, mountain upon mountain, patterns of catastrophe. He sips the coffee and it feels as if his insides are montainsides covered in snow, melting, and then abruptly he is collapsed on the floor, the curtains are folded away and collected in boxes, the room punctured, the man, holding all the stars, all the planets in place, ceiling caving in; the walls inside the body, subsiding, a devastation perhaps expected, though not yet, not like *this*. Machines plummet, light smothered by snow, the dry flakes of skin on the man's lower lip rejoin the flesh, pressed together like commuters packed on a train and starved of oxygen; a belt of everything implodes and combusts, the way grief can bring two people together.

We walk to the sea, and in one way we are a form waiting for collapse, in another we are that collapse already, at some other stage. You say a few things about how the war will proceed. How we should act. The crystallisation that is forever going on. Protest against the basic conditions, the refusal to even accept such terms. Everything else is madness, and worse: futile, without will.

And then again: the light of morning.

JOSEFINE KLOUGART (b. 1985) has been hailed as one of Denmark's greatest contemporary writers. Klougart is the author of five novels, two were nominated for the Nordic Council Literature Prize, Scandinavia's most prestigious literary award, and she received the Danish Royal Prize for Culture in 2011 with the committee stating that she is "one of the most important writers, not just of her generation, but of her time." Her English-language debut novel, *One of Us is Sleeping*, was published by Open Letter Books in 2016, also translated by Martin Aitken.

MARTIN AITKEN is an award-winning translator of Scandinavian literature. His translations include novels by authors such as Dorthe Nors, Peter Høeg, Helle Helle, and Pia Juul. He was awarded the American-Scandinavian Foundation's Nadia Christensen Translation Prize, and has been longlisted for both the Independent Foreign Fiction Prize and the IMPAC Dublin Literary Award. Aitken's co-translation with Don Bartlett of the sixth book in Karl Ove Knausgaard's *My Struggle* sextology is forthcoming in 2017.

Thank you all
for your support.
We do this for you,
and could not do
it without you.

DEEP
VELLUM

DEAR READERS,

Deep Vellum Publishing is a 501c3 nonprofit literary arts organization founded in 2013 with a threefold mission: to publish international literature in English translation; to foster the art and craft of translation; and to build a more vibrant book culture in Dallas and beyond. We are dedicated to broadening cultural connections across the English-reading world by connecting readers, in new and creative ways, with the work of international authors. We strive for diversity in publishing authors from various languages, viewpoints, genders, sexual orientations, countries, continents, and literary styles, whose works provide lasting cultural value and build bridges with foreign cultures while expanding our understanding of how the world thinks, feels, and experiences the human condition.

Operating as a nonprofit means that we rely on the generosity of tax-deductible donations from individual donors, cultural organizations, government institutions, and foundations. Your donations provide the basis of our operational budget as we seek out and publish exciting literary works from around the globe and build a vibrant and active literary arts community both locally and within the global society. Deep Vellum offers multiple donor levels, including LIGA DE ORO ($5,000+) and LIGA DEL SIGLO ($1,000+). Donors at various levels receive personalized benefits for their donations, including books and Deep Vellum merchandise, invitations to special events, and recognition in each book and on our website.

In addition to donations, we rely on subscriptions from readers like you to provide an invaluable ongoing investment in Deep Vellum that demonstrates a commitment to our editorial vision and mission. Subscribers are the bedrock of our support as we grow the readership for these amazing works of literature from every corner of the world. The investment our subscribers make allows us to demonstrate to potential donors and bookstores alike the support and demand for Deep Vellum's literature across a broad readership and gives us the ability to grow our mission in ever-new, ever-innovative ways.

In partnership with our sister company and bookstore, Deep Vellum Books, located in the historic cultural district of Deep Ellum in central Dallas, we organize and host literary programming such as author readings, translator workshops, creative writing classes, spoken word performances, and interdisciplinary arts events for writers, translators, and artists from across the globe. Our goal is to enrich and connect the world through the power of the written and spoken word, and we have been recognized for our efforts by being named one of the "Five Small Presses Changing the Face of the Industry" by *Flavorwire* and honored as Dallas's Best Publisher by *D Magazine*.

If you would like to get involved with Deep Vellum as a donor, subscriber, or volunteer, please contact us at deepvellum.org. We would love to hear from you.

Thank you all. Enjoy reading.
Will Evans Founder & Publisher Deep Vellum Publishing

LIGA DE ORO ($5,000+)

Anonymous (2)

LIGA DEL SIGLO ($1,000+)

Allred Capital Management
Ben & Sharon Fountain
David Tomlinson & Kathryn Berry
Judy Pollock
Life in Deep Ellum
Loretta Siciliano
Lori Feathers
Mary Ann Thompson-Frenk
& Joshua Frenk
Matthew Rittmayer
Meriwether Evans
Pixel and Texel
Nick Storch
Social Venture Partners Dallas
Stephen Bullock

DONORS

Adam Rekerdres
Alan Shockley
AMr.it Dhir
Anonymous
Andrew Yorke
Anthony Messenger
Bob Appel
Bob & Katherine Penn
Brandon Childress
Brandon Kennedy
Caroline Casey
Charles Dee Mitchell
Charley Mitcherson
Cheryl Thompson
Christie Tull
Daniel J. Hale

Ed Nawotka
Rev. Elizabeth
 & Neil Moseley
Ester & Matt Harrison
Grace Kenney
Greg McConeghy
Jeff Waxman
JJ Italiano
Justin Childress
Kay Cattarulla
Kelly Falconer
Linda Nell Evans
Lissa Dunlay
Marian Schwartz
 & Reid Minot
Mark Haber

Mary Cline
Maynard Thomson
Michael Reklis
Mike Kaminsky
Mokhtar Ramadan
Nikki & Dennis Gibson
Olga Kislova
Patrick Kukucka
Richard Meyer
Steve Bullock
Suejean Kim
Susan Carp
Susan Ernst
Theater Jones
Tim Perttula
Tony Thomson

SUBSCRIBERS

Anita Tarar

Ben Fountain

Ben Nichols

Blair Bullock

Bradford Pearson

Charles Dee Mitchell

Chris Sweet

Christie Tull

Courtney Sheedy

David Christensen

David Travis

David Weinberger

Dori Boone-Costantino

Elaine Corwin

Farley Houston

Frank Garrett

Guilty Dave Bristow

Horatiu Matei

James Tierney

Janine Allen

Jeanne Milazzo

Jeffrey Collins

Jessa Crispin

John O'Neill

John Schmerein

John Winkelman

Joshua Edwin

Kimberly Alexander

Kristopher Phillips

Marcia Lynx Qualey

Margaret Terwey

Martha Gifford

Meaghan Corwin

Michael Elliott

Michael Wilson

Mies de Vries

Mike Kaminsky

Neal Chuang

Nick Oxford

Nicola Molinaro

Patrick Shirak

Peter McCambridge

Stephanie Barr

Steven Kornajcik

Tim Kindseth

Tim Looney

Todd Jailer

Whitney Leader-Picone

Will Pepple

William Jarrell

AVAILABLE NOW FROM DEEP VELLUM

MICHÈLE AUDIN · *One Hundred Twenty-One Days*
translated by Christiana Hills · FRANCE

CARMEN BOULLOSA · *Texas: The Great Theft* · *Before*
translated by Samantha Schnee · translated by Peter Bush · MEXICO

LEILA S. CHUDORI · *Home*
translated by John H. McGlynn · INDONESIA

ALISA GANIEVA · *The Mountain and the Wall*
translated by Carol Apollonio · RUSSIA

ANNE GARRÉTA · *Sphinx*
translated by Emma Ramadan · FRANCE

JÓN GNARR · *The Indian* · *The Pirate*
translated by Lytton Smith· ICELAND

NOEMI JAFFE · *What are the Blind Men Dreaming?*
translated by Julia Sanches & Ellen Elias-Bursac · BRAZIL

JUNG YOUNG MOON · *Vaseline Buddha*
translated by Yewon Jung · SOUTH KOREA

FOUAD LAROUI · *The Curious Case of Dassoukine's Trousers*
translated by Emma Ramadan · MOROCCO

LINA MERUANE · *Seeing Red*
translated by Megan McDowell · CHILE

FISTON MWANZA MUJILA · *Tram 83*
translated by Roland Glasser · DEMOCRATIC REPUBLIC OF CONGO

ILJA LEONARD PFEIJFFER · *La Superba*
translated by Michele Hutchison · NETHERLANDS

RICARDO PIGLIA · *Target in the Night*
translated by Sergio Waisman · ARGENTINA

SERGIO PITOL · *The Art of Flight* · *The Journey*
translated by George Henson · MEXICO

MIKHAIL SHISHKIN · *Calligraphy Lesson: The Collected Stories*
translated by Marian Schwartz, Leo Shtutin,
Mariya Bashkatova, Sylvia Maizell · RUSSIA

SERHIY ZHADAN · *Voroshilovgrad*
translated by Reilly Costigan-Humes & Isaac Stackhouse Wheeler · UKRAINE

CARMEN BOULLOSA · *Heavens on Earth*
translated by Shelby Vincent · MEXICO

ANANDA DEVI · *Eve Out of Her Ruins*
translated by Jeffrey Zuckerman · MAURITIUS

JÓN GNARR · *The Outlaw*
translated by Lytton Smith· ICELAND

CLAUDIA SALAZAR JIMÉNEZ · *Blood of the Dawn*
translated by Elizabeth Bryer · PERU

JOSEFINE KLOUGART · *Of Darkness*
translated by Martin Aitken · DENMARK

SERGIO PITOL · *The Magician of Vienna*
translated by George Henson · MEXICO

EDUARDO RABASA · *A Zero-Sum Game*
translated by Christina MacSweeney · MEXICO

BAE SUAH · *Recitation*
translated by Deborah Smith · SOUTH KOREA

JUAN RULFO · *The Golden Cockerel & Other Writings*
translated by Douglas J. Weatherford · MEXICO

ANNE GARRÉTA · *Not One Day*
translated by Emma Ramadan · FRANCE

YANICK LAHENS · *Moonbath*
translated by Emily Gogolak · HAITI

DEEP
VELLUM